Friend. N...
When a n...
only a w...
he turns to Wife, Inc.

* * *

Please Let The New Nanny Be Some Dowdy Grandma Type Who Can Really Help Us,

Bryce thought, opening the door.

Her back to him, at first all he saw was a nicely rounded behind tucked inside jeans, a white blouse and a brown leather vest. And chestnut-brown hair pulled up in a ponytail. Not exactly grandma, he thought.

Then the woman turned, and staring him in the face was the one woman, the only woman, who'd rocked his world and set it on fire. "What are you doing here?"

"I'm from Wife, Incorporated." Her brows knitted slightly. "Weren't you expecting me?"

"I was expecting someone, certainly not you."

"Life is full of little surprises, huh?"

He wanted to call Wife, Incorporated, and ask for someone less...beautiful and exotic. But he needed help now. Besides, he could handle this. He wasn't going to get involved with the nanny, no matter who she was....

Dear Reader,

Summer vacation is simply a state of mind...so create your dream getaway by reading six new love stories from Silhouette Desire!

Begin your romantic holiday with *A Cowboy's Pursuit* by Anne McAllister. This MAN OF THE MONTH title is the author's 50th book and part of her CODE OF THE WEST miniseries. Then learn how a Connelly bachelor mixes business with pleasure in *And the Winner Gets...Married!* by Metsy Hingle, the sixth installment of our exciting DYNASTIES: THE CONNELLYS continuity series.

An unlikely couple swaps insults and passion in Maureen Child's *The Marine & the Debutante*—the latest of her popular BACHELOR BATTALION books. And a night of passion ignites old flames in *The Bachelor Takes a Wife* by Jackie Merritt, the final offering in TEXAS CATTLEMAN'S CLUB: THE LAST BACHELOR continuity series.

In *Single Father Seeks...* by Amy J. Fetzer, a businessman and his baby captivate a CIA agent working under cover as their nanny. And in Linda Conrad's *The Cowboy's Baby Surprise,* an amnesiac FBI agent finds an undreamed-of happily-ever-after when he's reunited with his former partner and lover.

Read these passionate, powerful and provocative new Silhouette Desire romances and enjoy a sensuous summer vacation!

Joan Marlow Golan

Joan Marlow Golan
Senior Editor, Silhouette Desire

Please address questions and book requests to:
Silhouette Reader Service
U.S.: 3010 Walden Ave., P.O. Box 1325, Buffalo, NY 14269
Canadian: P.O. Box 609, Fort Erie, Ont. L2A 5X3

Single Father Seeks...

AMY J. FETZER

Silhouette®

Desire®

Published by Silhouette Books

America's Publisher of Contemporary Romance

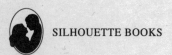 SILHOUETTE BOOKS

ISBN 0-373-76445-6

SINGLE FATHER SEEKS...

AMY J. FETZER

was born in New England and raised all over the world. She uses her own experiences in creating the characters and settings for her novels. Married more than twenty years to a United States Marine and the mother of two sons, Amy covets the moments when she can curl up with a cup of cappuccino and a good book.

Dedicated with love to my son, Zackary Cain,

For your cartoon obsessions and wanting to explore
and invent and draw. For likely being the only teenager
who does what he's told when he's told and doing it
well. For having big dreams and a natural kindness
that only angels possess. You, my son, have made me
grow as a person and understand why a mother
would gladly lay down her life for her child.
I love you.

Prologue

Hong Kong

He was Secret Service. She was CIA. He wasn't hiding that fact.

She was.

But right now they weren't hiding a thing from each other. A desire, no, a raging passion she'd never imagined existed inside her, was taking complete command. Ciara loved every second of it. And from the look on his face as she shoved open his trousers, so did he.

She drove her hand inside the dark fabric and he groaned and pushed her against the nearest wall, taking her mouth with an excitement so powerful, so hot, it would burn out of control in no time. She was counting on it. She had wanted him the minute she saw him. She wanted to be wild and escape and spend this one night with him. He was head-turning handsome with a hard body, and that sexy to-die-for look of a secret agent. Coal-black hair, Nordic blue eyes, and a chiseled jaw she wanted to kiss 'til dawn. Add to that a gentlemanly southern drawl, slightly disguised, and she was melting for him with the first word.

Behind them in the hotel room lay a trail of clothes—black, inconspicuous. Just what their jobs called for. But the situation now called for none. Naked. Ciara was nearly there. He wasn't getting there soon enough.

He ground against her, letting her know he was ready for whatever she had in mind, and she pushed his trousers lower and cupped the tight curve of his buttocks, pulling him into her and sending the same message.

"You're driving me insane, you know that?" he said, his voice whiskey rough as his mouth rolled over her throat, her shoulder. He made quick work of her slip, adding it to the trail with her dress.

"No more than you are me."

He unclasped her bra, pulling it off, tossing it aside, then filling his palms with her breasts.

Ciara gasped, then gasped again as his thumbs circled her nipples deeply. Oh mercy, his touch was all she needed to explode.

"The instant I saw you, I thought about this."

She smiled. "Did you imagine this?" she asked, then slicked her tongue over his nipple. He flinched and made a helpless sound she already loved.

"Yeah, I did."

His knife-creased black slacks hit the floor, and she bent to help them all the way off. And when she stood, she scrubbed her hands over his corded thighs, his trim bare hips. He was built like a wall of muscle, twisted, ropy, delicious to touch and she could tell that he liked watching her touch him. It made her burn for more. She wrapped her hand around his arousal and stroked him harder than he already was.

He couldn't take it and suddenly he grabbed her against him, and growled, "My turn." He knelt, peeling her panties down as he went and just the motion made her breathless. He laid wet, grinding kisses to every inch of skin he exposed, rolled her thigh-high stockings down like unrolling a piece of candy and he murmured, "I had a sneaky feeling you were wearing these."

Just knowing she had, in a roomful of attachés and dignitaries and the former first lady, drove him wild. Now she was wearing only a strand of pearls.

"My, my, secret agent man. You were fantasizing a lot more than I thought," she said, then howled when his mouth covered her soft center. He licked and played, probed and stroked until she was biting her lip to keep from screaming and bringing hotel security. For an instant, a sliver of time, she wondered about letting a complete stranger do this to her, then she didn't care. He was all she'd imagined and more, and when he threw her leg over his shoulder and drove deeper, Ciara thought she'd come apart at the seams.

He chuckled darkly as she melted, her leg slipping limply off his shoulder as she sank down, sliding down the wall and straddling his thighs.

"There's a bed a few feet away," he said.

"Too far," she gasped, rocking against his thickness.

He reached for his trousers, fumbled in the pocket, and she barely noticed because he never took his mouth from her. He bent her back over his arm, and then he was inside her, driving upward and clasping her against his wide chest.

"Oh, sweet heaven," he groaned, cupping her bottom and giving her hips motion because he couldn't stop it. Bryce pushed his fingers into her hair, loving the sounds she made, that she was as demanding as he, because he craved her. *Craved.* He'd never hungered for a woman from first sight, never had instant fantasies and instant arousal as he had with just looking at her. The moment he spotted her in that plain black dress, standing off to the side, he'd been preoccupied with her. Wondering what was under that simple dress, enjoying the shift of silk as she walked. Wondering what she looked like with her hair down instead of in that tight, reserved twist. He even liked the way she sipped champagne. And the way she looked at him, slow and possessive. As if she knew what he looked like naked, and she was in a hurry to see it firsthand. As if she knew one touch and they'd be unrestrained and reckless like this.

No one would have suspected. She had an innocence in her face, a cheerleader all-American scrubbed clean look, but a body like a movie star. All woman, ripe and curvy. Not skinny and flat. He loved it. And knew, even if she wasn't rocking against him, that he held a real woman in his arms. A woman who enjoyed being a woman. And he wanted to do nothing but see pleasure on her beautiful face.

Bryce got down to the business of giving her exactly what she wanted and tasted every inch of her he could reach, stroked her, nipped and soothed and discovered the backs of her thighs were extremely sensitive. Then suddenly, they were over the top, thrashing against each other, rolling across the lush carpet. In the space of a few minutes they tried three positions, laughing as they contorted, then gasping when the friction was almost too much to bear, hurrying, taking only seconds for a thick kiss, and when he had her beneath him, vulnerable, he pushed into her with a measured deliberation that made her cry out and claw for him. She locked her legs around his hips and thrust and pulsed, touching him everywhere, and he held her off the floor, pushing and retreating, watching her pleasure ignite over her exquisite features. He would take that moment with him forever, he thought. Never had he been with a woman who was so confident in herself, in her sexuality, and it made him want her more. She gave as much as she took.

Then it came.

The heavy rush of heat and sensation, a tingling so intense it felt like needles on his spine. Like a throbbing wave about to crash. Suddenly she gripped his jaw and whispered, "Take me with you," and he pushed, once, twice, and they reached for the stars together.

She cried out and bowed like a ribbon of womanly passion.

Time stopped. Soft moans and panting breaths filling the expensive hotel room. Moonlight spilled through the windows and coated them as his desire beat a throbbing pulse inside her, stretching as her feminine muscles flexed and pawed around him.

Bryce looked down at her, trembling with the power of their loving and she smiled up at him, pulling his weight onto her. She was barely sated, her foot sliding up his calf, his thigh, her hands stroking him, holding him as if she'd known him all her life and not just the past few hours.

With a hard sigh, he rolled to his side, tucking her close, yet before they could catch their breath, pagers went off, a cell phone rang.

He kissed her deeply. "Ignore them."

"I can't." But she kissed him back anyway, then disentangled herself from him.

He rose up, reaching for her. "Where are you going?"

"I have to answer that." She knew from experience that whoever was on the other end of that line would not give up. "Don't want hotel security coming up and asking why we're still making so much noise, right?"

He didn't give a damn. He wanted her again.

But she was already going for the phone, gathering her clothes as she talked softly. She looked back at him, and he let his gaze roam her naked body, to the deep chestnut brown hair spilling down her back. Man, she was luscious. She smiled, returning the stare with equal intensity. He felt himself grow hard again. Then she slipped into the bathroom and closed the door.

Bryce looked around at the debris of clothes, and

started to reach for them, then gave up and fell onto the carpet.

He'd never done anything like that before. Never.

A total stranger. A siren in a little black dress and pearls.

Less than five minutes later she came out of the bathroom, fully dressed and pulling on the strappy little sandals that made him want to taste her ankles. She walked to him and stopped. He hadn't moved. Good grief, he could still scarcely breathe.

"I have to go," she said and her eyes were all business.

"Now?"

Her sudden smile was small and purely feminine. "Yeah. No strings remember?"

"And no names."

She tipped her head to the side. "It's better this way. You have an important job and I'd just be a complication."

"Just who the hell are you?"

"An embassy secretary."

"Liar."

Her expression, one that had been so open with emotion minutes ago, slammed closed. Cold. Detached. And making him think that the woman standing before him now was a ghost of the passionate creature he'd held in his arms. He didn't like it.

She tossed him his pager, and he caught it. "The first lady is calling you."

He looked at the pager and wondered how she could tell from just a number. Or was that just an educated guess? Most Secret Service agents in a crowd didn't look very secretive. When he looked up, she was lowering onto his lap, her arms wrapping his neck. Her mouth played over his with a heat that seared him again.

Now *this* was the woman he wanted to be with. ''Can I interest you in another round, darlin'?'' he said against her lips as his hands moved under the hem of her dress.

What a temptation, to discard her duties and have another romp with this hunk of man. But her partner needed her. ''You could *always* interest me, secret agent man. But, I have to go.''

She stood, bent to kiss him once more, leaving her scent branded into his skin, and he lay there like an idiot and watched her walk out of his life. Forever. He knew it was forever. Excitement like that was once in a lifetime and neither of them, obviously had the time or the will to grab hold and keep it. Bryce had a feeling that the lady in black was just a dream and none of this was real.

One

Five years later
Beaufort, South Carolina

Ciara needed to hide. To go deep under.

In a spot not even the CIA would think to look.

The world was a big place. She could be anywhere, right?

And this small southern town was just the right ticket. It was historical and touristy. If need be, she could blend in. A CIA safe house, a cabin in the wilderness would have been better, but she'd have to go through agency contacts to get one and Ciara wasn't trusting anyone just yet.

She'd already trusted the wrong man, she thought with a cynical twist to her lips and a glance in the rearview mirror to see if she were being followed. And that's the reason she was dropping out of sight.

She blamed most of that on herself. With the exception of a one-night affair five years ago, she'd been burned enough by men whose job it was to lie and deceive and gain crucial information. When did she get so clueless about them? When had she refused to believe a thing a man said? Gee, she thought. Maybe when her partner started showing up late for rendezvous and had more cash than they earned in a year. And the worst of this was, that two years ago they'd been lovers. Though it was long over, she'd let old feelings interfere with her judgment, and didn't see what was really going on. And it had taken her a while to admit it. He'd used her emotionally and professionally, and that she'd allowed it to happen was too humiliating to swallow. She'd never make that mistake again. Not with any man.

Her hand slipped off the wheel and touched the flight tote with the videotape stashed inside. It was backup, and she thought of the man she'd caught betraying his country on the film. Her partner, Mark Faraday was six feet of slender male, with sunbleached hair that told her he had more time off than she did. Good-looking, but not too good-looking to draw attention, Mark was born with a silver tongue. Now the laid back surfer spy was a national security risk by giving classified material away. A mole. And a risk to her.

She made a sour face and for the tenth time, called herself a fool. Then she'd called in a favor from her old college sorority sister, Katherine Davenport. First, Kat had been shocked to hear from her after all these years, and second, reluctant to give her a job. But Ciara would go nuts if she were stashed somewhere with nothing to do, waiting for the truth to come out and drag Mark to a high-security prison. She had to keep occupied, and her mind off her troubles. Caring for a one-year-old girl was going to be easy, like reliving her teen years. She'd practically raised her little sister Cassie after their parents had been killed in a jet crash over Scotland. Well, she and her older brothers. It hadn't taken much to convince Kat she was qualified. Childcare was how she'd earned extra money during college. Ciara knew baby care about as well as she knew when and where the satellites were aligned to pick up the best frequencies and take aerial photos.

Ciara had to assure Kat she wasn't putting anyone in danger. And the first thing she would do when she had a chance was mail the videotape to a neutral party. Then a carefully worded note that would take the heat off of her.

She wasn't paying much attention to the beautiful landscape until she hit a rut in the road. She braked, gawking at the gnarled live oaks draped in Spanish moss and the so-green-it-hurt-her-eyes lawn. The scent of jasmine came through the car's air conditioner, enveloping her. Throwing the car into park, she quickly climbed out, checking the address, then stared at the house.

House?

Heck, this was *Tara* revisited. Two stories with wraparound porches on both levels, the white house was magnificent—spreading across an acre and surrounded by about ten more, if she had to guess.

Did only a widower and a baby live in all this?

She hoped he had a maid.

Grabbing her tote, she slung it onto her shoulder and walked up the steps, taking a deep breath of the fragrances of jasmine and wisteria. An odd peace came with it, and the tension she'd carried for days flowed out of her muscles.

This wasn't just isolation and safety, this was a dream.

Bryce felt warm slimy peaches slide off his face and plop on his chest. "Well," he said tiredly, staring blankly at his eleven-month-old daughter. "I see we're going to have to work on your table etiquette."

She shrieked, twisting her head to the side when he offered her more. Bryce tossed the spoon aside and sagged into the chair, giving up this battle.

Carolina proceeded to play with the mess on the high chair tray.

Bryce looked around at the results of feeding his daughter and knew his late wife was laughing. Diana would say this was justice for not loving her like she needed. God knows he had tried. He'd done everything he could to make the marriage work. A marriage he hadn't wanted. She'd loved him, but in the end, he knew she'd hated him.

Guilt swam through Bryce. He and Diana had been lovers briefly when he'd come home from the Secret Service for a visit. Those two nights produced the little girl in the high chair. And when Carolina had arrived, Diana's life ended. He loved his baby more than his life, and he knew that marrying Diana because she was pregnant was the right thing to do then, but he hadn't mourned her.

The guilt intensified and he pushed his fingers into his hair and pushed the thoughts out of his mind.

He swore he was never going to get involved with a woman again.

Heck, he was terrified of letting *this* tiny female down. Of ruining her life like he had her mother's. He couldn't trust himself not to destroy another woman's life. Not to mention the damage it did to his soul.

His daughter flung the mushy beige food, a glob landing on his shirt. He didn't bother to wipe it and thought of his former colleagues in the Secret Service seeing him now. A far cry from the man who lived dangerously, moment to moment protecting the first family. He was now Mr. Mom and a complete failure at it, he thought. There should be a school or something for dads who had to be moms, too.

Four days without a nanny and he was seeing exactly how useless he was at being a reliable father. He didn't think he'd miss the skills of a woman more than he did right now. His sister had helped him a few times after Diana's death, but she had her own family. His parents were retired, leaving him the family business and this monstrous house while they traveled the world. It was only right, but the shrimping business was taking off like a runaway train and he hadn't been able to operate it from this house since before his daughter was born.

He looked at his baby. He'd had a nanny, but she'd refused to be a live-in. Carolina needed consistency, someone there for her when he couldn't be. Someone who would be tender and loving. And almost a mother. What his baby didn't need was a parade of strangers marching through her life now. She was so young and had a tendency to scream bloody murder when a stranger got close. Probably because all she ever saw was him and the nanny. The maid, well she was from a service, and all business. And rarely the same one each time.

The last nanny said Carolina was difficult. And when he'd found the woman lounging around, watching soap operas while his daughter cried in a playpen, Bryce had fired her. The next three nannies hadn't been any better.

Neglecting his child was not an option, nor was putting her in a day-care center where she'd get sick and there were too many children. He wanted his daughter to have attention while he was at work. Lord, he didn't think finding child care would be so difficult. Luckily, someone had recommended Wife Incorporated to him. He'd spoken with the owner, Katherine Davenport, and though she sounded nice, what mattered was that she'd come to his rescue. She was sending a nanny out today. Any minute.

Bryce prayed it was someone with a tender heart.

And he hoped she arrived soon.

Carolina shrieked, her lip curling down, and he left his chair to walk over to a cookie jar. He gave her one cookie. Instantly she quieted.

He would deal with the chocolate mess later.

Bribery, he thought as he dropped back into the chair, was acceptable in grave situations.

Bryce started to clean up the mess, bending down on his hands and knees to get the food spilled on the floor. He chased a piece of cereal and when Carolina burst into tears, he flinched and bumped his head on the table. He stood, staring down at her as she reared back in that squirm he'd come to know meant she was done and wanted down now. Then she started kicking and crying. Bryce rushed to finish cleaning up the mess, then handed his daughter a carrot to grind against her cutting teeth.

"Five minutes, princess," he pleaded. "I just need five minutes."

She threw the carrot and cried harder.

Then the doorbell rang.

Taking Carolina out of the high chair, Bryce struggled to keep a safe hold on her when she squirmed, refusing to be still. Since she was already climbing out of her crib and crawling away with amazing speed, he didn't dare put her on the floor yet. Besides, he could tell how clean it wasn't anyway.

"We have company, sweetie." Carolina looked up at him, chocolate cookie smeared over her face and clothes. She worked the mush in her hand as if it would hurry it into her mouth. Then she stilled and offered him a bite, missing his mouth and jamming the soggy cookie somewhere near his ear.

"Well," he said as he walked toward the door. "Guess it's good that she sees us at our worst, huh?"

His hand on the door, Bryce tipped his head back. *Please Lord, let it be some dowdy grandma type who can really help us.*

He opened the door.

Her back to him, at first all he saw was a nicely rounded behind tucked inside jeans, a white blouse and a brown leather vest. And chestnut-brown hair pulled up in a ponytail.

Not exactly grandma, he thought.

The woman turned and her features slackened.

Bryce thought his knees would fold beneath him any second.

Staring him in the face was the one woman, the only woman, who'd rocked his world and set it on fire.

"I can't believe this," he said more to himself.

"Well, hey there, secret agent man," she replied softly and the words held the echo of the one and only time they'd been together.

Bryce's body seized with the memory. Naked and wild. The feel and taste of her rocketing through his mind. "What are you doing here?"

"I'm from Wife Incorporated." Her brows knitted slightly. "Weren't you expecting me?"

"I was expecting someone, certainly not you."

"Life is full of little surprises, huh?"

Surprise, hell. This was a "knock him into next week" shock, he thought, holding her gaze and seeing much more in her cognac-brown eyes, the way they flared when he was inside her, the sly look she got when she knew she was giving him pleasure.

And Ciara saw it, in his expression, the memory of that one night. She swallowed hard, trying to keep her cool and not remember the only time she'd seen this man...when he had her up against a hotel wall and was devouring her. Greedy and primal. The instant their eyes met, her body had jumped to life. Now she felt her breathing increase, heat twisting through her. He was the only man who could do that to her. With just a look of those ice-blue eyes.

And now she was suppose to live in his house?

Her gaze swept him. He looked ragged, and far

from the man she saw last. Baby food clung to his hair and T-shirt, and there was a dark brown streak hastily wiped off his cheek near his ear. His jeans were splattered with assorted bits of soggy cereal and spilled coffee. It was almost comical, except in his arms a dark haired infant was twisting like a slippery fish trying to get back in the water, and crying to be let down.

Ciara instantly dropped her bag and stepped closer. "Hey," she said softly, tugging on the baby's dress, which was in as bad a shape as her father's shirt and slacks. "Hey there."

The baby came upright sharply and stared at her with wide blue eyes. "Hello there, sweetie," she said, her gaze on the child as she asked, "Are you going to introduce me, Mr. Bryce Ashland?"

Bryce blinked and followed her gaze to Carolina, who was still crying, but looking curious. His gaze shot back to her. "Maybe when I know your name."

Smiling, she held out her hand. "Ciara. Ciara Stuart."

Bryce grasped her hand and the pulse of her blood hummed through him. Oh God, he thought. It hasn't changed one bit. One touch and his entire being jumped to life, his nerves jingling and leaving his heart thumping like a sledgehammer in his chest. Everything he remembered about her came back tenfold and Bryce realized in that moment that this woman had done more than leave an impression.

She'd branded him.

It was so strong that Hong Kong seemed like days ago, not five years.

Her memory was just as clear, and Ciara's heart

skipped into high gear, the warmth of his fingers around hers reminding her of how seductive they could be. How they felt on her skin, slipping inside her body. Suddenly she ached with a longing so deep she had trouble not groaning aloud. Just looking at him made her feel alive and hot. Her secret agent man. Her fantasy man. Oh, this was too weird. A shock, yes, a danger, maybe. How was she going to be around this man? Especially when all she could think of was that seductive night and that in those few short hours he'd made feel more alive and female and wicked than in her entire life. Or that the memory of him had kept her company when she was isolated and completely friendless.

Her fingers moved in his and his grip tightened warmly. For a moment she thought he'd lace his fingers with hers and pull her toward him like he'd done in the elevator that night. As if he understood, he gave her a sexy smile that made her toes curl, then pulled free.

Bryce inclined his head. "This is my daughter, Carolina."

Ciara dragged her attention back to the baby and noticed the brown goo all over her. "Chocolate?" Her eyes went wide. "For a baby? Are you nuts? Oh, you do need help." She lightly clapped her hands, then held them out to the child.

Carolina launched into her arms. The crying instantly stopped.

Ciara patted the baby's back, and Bryce watched in complete amazement as his daughter nuzzled her dirty face against Ciara's chest.

Bryce blinked. "It's got to be a woman thing."

"Not really, it's a baby thing. I'm just not fighting with her." She grinned at him, a little devilish and his heart choked. "Besides, she's warm, messy, sticky and I can't believe you gave her sugar." She plucked the remains of the cookie from the baby and dropped it into his hand.

Carolina didn't make a fuss. Then Ciara stepped inside the house, brushing past him. "Which way to the kitchen?" she said as she walked.

"Your next right." He stood there for a moment, then grabbed her bag and her suitcases off the porch and brought them inside. Closing the door, he strode into the kitchen, tossing the cookie in the trash.

She had Carolina on the counter and was gently washing her face and hands, talking softly, smiling. "Well, darling, you need a bath and some fresh clothes." She glanced at Bryce, then her gaze swept meaningfully to the mess on the kitchen table. "How much of that did she really eat?"

"Not much. She more or less made missiles of it all."

Ciara nodded. "Does she use a bottle or a cup?"

"As of recently, one of these," he said, holding up a tippy cup that rolled when he set it back down.

"Is she on a schedule?"

"A what?"

Lifting the child in her arms, she looked at him. He was washing his hands, and not more than two feet away from her. It set her nerves tingling again.

"A schedule. Nap time, bedtime, bath time."

"No."

"So she's been ruling the roost."

His shoulder sagged a little. "Pretty much." Why

did that embarrass him? Drying his hands on a towel, he eyed her. "You aren't going to regiment Carolina into a routine, are you?"

"No, but I've learned from the best that setting times for meals and naps helps babies as much as it does the parents." She cocked her head. "How do you think moms get anything done?"

"It's a talent that has escaped me, obviously." He cleared his throat and asked, "Are you a mother?"

"No, and never married."

He nodded. "So how did you get experience with babies?"

"I have all the requirements you wanted, but I raised my younger sister and I earned money in college by being a nanny. Mostly on the weekends, though."

"Made for dull college days."

"I wouldn't say that." She looked at the baby in her arms, realizing that it had been a while since she'd cared for a child this young. Years. Since she'd joined the agency. Yet the memories of her college years swept through her like a warm, gentle breeze. Those other people's children had been her saviors when she'd felt lonely and homesick. And though she never considered herself mom material, especially after years with the CIA, this child needed her. It was obvious with the chaos in this house. But could she be objective, walk away when everything in her career was back to normal?

"Ms. Stuart?"

Bryce's tone warned her that he'd called her more than once and she blamed her inattention on the alias last name she'd given him. She met his gaze and smiled. "Call me Ciara. I think it's a bit more appropriate."

His features tightened, as if fighting a smile.

"She looks just like you," Ciara said and somehow that pleased him.

He looked at his daughter and his entire body softened. He moved closer, touching Carolina's hair. "You think so?"

"Yeah."

He met her gaze and their close proximity made his thoughts skip and stall on her, made him imagine what she looked like naked. What she felt like in his arms. This was going to be tough if he couldn't even look at her without remembering that night. He wanted to call Wife Incorporated and ask for someone less...beautiful and exotic. But he needed help now. Besides, he could handle this, he thought. He wasn't going to get involved with the nanny, no matter who she was. However, just seeing his baby cuddled in her arms did something to him.

"So Mr. Ashland, are we going to stand in this tornado of a room all day or are you going to show me this house and tell me what I'll be doing?"

Bryce watched her stroke Carolina's arm, then press her lips to the top of his daughter's head. As if she'd known his child from the day she was born. But household duties were not what he was thinking about right now. He couldn't take his eyes off Ciara. She hadn't changed. She was still a classic beauty, and though she looked a little thinner than before, she was still curved and womanly. The thought of putting his hands on her bare skin again made him hard, and he instantly knew he could get into real trouble with her around. He reminded himself she was his employee and old fantasies were just that. Old and buried. Well, he thought with a long look at her, not quite buried.

Before his imagination took off to parts unknown, he cleared his throat and gestured to the room. "The kitchen obviously," he tossed a thumb back over his shoulder. "The garage, laundry room and back door are that way. There's an old servants staircase there, too."

Servant. That's what she was to him. Even if he was looking at her like they'd made love last night instead of five years ago. And despite that and the fantasies floating through her mind when she looked at him, she had to keep that in mind, remember why she was here and that she'd be leaving soon. It wouldn't take the agency long to nab Mark.

Needing a distraction, Ciara looked around the huge peach, green and white kitchen. It was decorated like something out of a magazine, with all the latest appliances and an island counter with a sink. A chef's dream. She couldn't wait to see the rest of this place.

"Can you cook?"

"Sure." She frowned a bit. "With Wife Incorporated, it's a requirement. Why would you ask?"

"Home cooking is the last thing I'd expect from you," he said with a sly glance.

Ciara's heart skipped an entire beat at the sound of his voice and she looked him over. "Being a dad is the last I'd have expected of you."

He gave her a velvety look. "No expectations, remember?"

She smirked. How could she *not* remember?

Bryce walked ahead and with the baby in her arms,

Ciara followed him into the living room. "Front parlor," he said, then pointed out the dining room beyond before walking into the main hall. The foyer was wide, a staircase on the right sweeping to the second floor. He pointed to it. "Bedrooms and baths upstairs, den and library there," he said, gesturing to the left as he walked down the hall.

Carolina made noises, adding her own input.

Now that she'd had the chance to really look, Ciara was floored. The carved ceiling panels and wainscoting were works of art. Paintings hung on the walls and the hall was wide enough to fit a settee. When she'd driven up the long oak tree-lined driveway and had first seen the two-story house with double porches, she wondered how she was supposed to take care of this place when it went on forever. White with green plantation shutters, it spoke of old charm and grace, and she admitted it gave her a strange sense of home.

Odd, when she hadn't had a real home since joining the CIA.

He led her back through the kitchen, then into a large Carolina room banked with windows and filled with casual furniture, the TV, a stereo. He crossed to a pair of French doors and threw them open, letting her step out onto the back deck first.

And as she passed he whispered softly, "Welcome, Ciara, to *River Bend*."

Two

Ciara stilled for a second. His tone made it seem as if he'd waited a lifetime to say that. And he meant it. She didn't dare look back over her shoulder at him. She could already feel the heat of his muscled body behind her like the sweet warmth of the sun. The urge to stop and sink back into him was nearly overpowering.

She mentally shook herself. Fantasy ends here, she thought. She hated that just his presence gave her ideas she'd no business having. She stepped farther onto the back deck and said, "Thank you. So, you named your house?"

He eyed her. "I take it you're not from the south."

Finally, she looked at him. "Well, I could fake a southern accent, if you want." She couldn't tell him that yes, she was from the south, born and raised only a couple hundred miles away from here, but she'd taken great pains to lose her southern accent. In the CIA, it didn't help to have her speech marked so clearly.

They walked farther out onto the deck.

Ciara scanned the landscape and lost her breath. "My God, this is heaven."

Though they were a good hundred yards from the water, the view was incredible—the river, houses on the other side, the sea toward the inlet. There was an in-ground pool and beyond it a gazebo big enough to house a table and chairs and chaise lounges. Live oaks and palm trees shaded the yard here and there, and even as the sun began its descent, she could see an intricate flower garden off to the left, a wicker sofa and table tucked under the spreading branches dripping with Spanish moss. That same sense of peace swept her again and her gaze landed on a wood swing hanging from a tree limb, and then a babbling fountain resting under the shade trees. Ahead of her, a dock stretched for half the length of a football field over the marsh to the water, a screened porch lay a few yards before the end of the pier. There were two boats anchored at the end, a dinged-up, well-used johnboat and a ritzy gleaming cabin cruiser. The contrast spoke volumes about Bryce.

"All this from the Secret Service?" she said softly.

He chuckled to himself. "Lord no. I barely made the rent working for the government. This house has been in my family for generations. It was my parents' home."

"They're retired?"

"Yes, they live in Florida when they aren't on a jet heading somewhere else."

She looked at the baby, rocking her from side to side and noticing her little eyelids drooping. "A lot of house for just the two of you, huh sweetheart?" When she looked at Bryce, he was staring at her oddly. Her brows knit, her look questioning.

Bryce couldn't say why he was so touched by the gesture. His baby in her arms, the gentle way Ciara touched Carolina. He never expected anything so tender from a woman like her. And he reminded himself that all he knew about her was what it was like to make love to her, to be completely and utterly driven mad by her touch.

Stop looking at me like that, she wanted to say, but she didn't want to open that can of worms.

"It's breathtaking," she said into the silence. "Did you grow up here?"

"Yes. Me and my sister Hope. She lives closer to town." Bryce looked off at the marsh. "There are gators in there occasionally. If you go near, be careful."

"I understand." She kept her gaze on the landscape as they strolled around the pool deck. "The décor is lovely, Bryce. Who did it? Your wife?"

He looked at her sharply. "No, my mother. I didn't live here with Diana."

She propped Carolina on her hip and said, "Diana, huh?"

The mention of his wife's name set him suddenly on edge. "I wasn't married to her when you and I met."

Her brows shot up. "I didn't think you were." A pause and then, "So what happened to her?"

A surge of guilt pounded through Bryce at the thought of his late wife, and what he'd done to her life. He didn't want to talk about Diana. Especially not with Ciara. Somehow, if he did, it felt as if he were hurting Diana more than he already had.

At his hesitation she added, "If it's too painful and you'd rather not…"

"Yes, it is painful, but—" He gave Ciara the minimum. "She died when Carolina was born. She had gestational diabetes. The pregnancy was very difficult. Toxemia and the diabetes caused her death."

Ciara heard the anger building in his voice. And the torment in his features. He must have loved his wife deeply, she thought. To lose his wife and then be forced to care for a newborn alone, how hard it must have been for him.

In the ensuing silence, she watched him stare out over the marsh, his handsome features twisted with anger and the echo of old pain.

"And while we are on the subject, let's get one thing straight right now," he said, grinding the words past clenched teeth. He faced her, his hands on his hips, his entire stance as belligerent as a man about to do battle. Something had changed in him in those few seconds, with those few words. Gone was the sexy man she knew, the man needing help with his child, and before her stood a guardian. Guarding what, she didn't know.

"I'm listening."

"I'm not looking for a replacement."

She blinked. "I'm not looking to be one." She had

a career to return to, a job that meant changing the world.

"Carolina is my concern. She needs someone who is here when I'm not. She needs...mothering."

Oh lord, Ciara thought. Baby-sitting yes, but mothering? After years with the CIA, she was the farthest thing from a mother type. Was she out of her league with this job? Too late to back out now, she thought, remembering how she'd badgered Katherine into giving her this position. Take it like an undercover assignment, she thought, a masquerade. "I can handle it."

He eyed her. "I know you're bonded and trained, but that has little to do with caring for my daughter."

"I should say so." Did he think she was completely incapable?

Silence. Hard and biting as they stared.

She squared off with him, wondering why he was suddenly so defensive. "Why don't you just say what's on your mind, Bryce? Get it off your chest right now."

"I don't trust you." There was just too much mystery surrounding her. The fact that she was back in his life, in this position, was enough to make him cautious.

"You did enough that night." Instantly she hated herself for bringing up their past.

"That was five years ago. I was single without a care except who was looking funny at the former first lady. And that night was just about us. Now it's about Carolina." He shook his head. "My life is completely different. I'm not the same man."

"Well, here's a news flash, Ashland. I haven't

changed. I'm not the mother type. I'll do my level best for Carolina while I'm here, but don't expect what I can't give."

Bryce recognized her look. Her features shuttered so quickly he felt it like a cold breeze. It was the same look she'd given him in the hotel room when she'd come out of the bathroom, dressed and ready to leave. All traces of the passion they'd shared were erased.

That she could hold his baby in her arms and could call on this emotionless look, added to his suspicions. "What were you doing in Hong Kong?"

"Embassy work." It wasn't a lie, she thought, just not the whole truth. "Now can I have a say?"

He nodded.

"What happened between us was a one-time thing. One time. This is a coincidence, a one in a million chance. Deal with it. I need the job, and you and Carolina need me. Let's just leave it at that, okay, *boss?*"

"My daughter needs you, not me."

"Thanks for clarifying that," she said. "I was having visions of weddings and receptions already."

Her delivery was cold and sarcastic. Bryce didn't like it.

"And while we're drawing battle lines, if I'd wanted more after Hong Kong, I would have looked you up again," she said. "Really great sex doesn't mean I want a lifetime."

His features yanked taut.

"Have I made *myself* clear?"

He nodded. "Fine. We understand each other."

"Not by a long shot, Ashland."

Bryce's lips tightened.

She arched a brow. Let him stew, she thought. She wouldn't be revealing anything about herself or her past, and that one night with him had nothing to do with the present. Except to remind her that while his life had changed and grown, hers hadn't. All that was different was the one mistake she'd made. Trusting the wrong man. The instant she thought of her partner and the magnitude of his betrayal, Ciara knew she couldn't trust her feelings. About anything. She'd botched it up badly by not seeing what was there, and with Bryce, she had to remember the price of loving—no, not love, the price of getting involved with someone had only rewarded Ciara with heartache. Besides she had to lie to him, she had to keep her real life secret. Involving him in any part of her career or the knowledge of it could bring harm to him or this sweet baby. She would never allow that to happen. She'd vanish first. Her job was to protect her country's interests—and its people were under that umbrella.

Even if it was raining where she stood.

"I'll put your bags in your room," Bryce said, effectively ending this standoff, "and your car in the garage."

She fished in the pocket of her jeans and tossed him the keys, glad she'd cleared the rental car of anything that bore her real name. "I'll be with your daughter." She turned sharply and headed back into the house.

"Where are you going?"

"The sun is too hot for her without a bonnet and sunblock, and she's tired."

Bryce silently approved and followed, then frowned at her back as she walked briskly through the house toward the foyer. Though she held his daughter gently, allowing Carolina to grab onto her ponytail, he could feel the remoteness about Ciara. It was as if she had an invisible wall around her now.

He didn't blame her, really. And it was better for him all around. But for his daughter? Though her actions toward his baby so far were tender, Bryce wondered if she'd deny Carolina her affections because of him.

It was another reason not to trust her.

He'd have to keep an eye on her for the next few days.

And nights?

Damn.

The thought of this woman sleeping down the hall from him made his body jump and rock to life.

"I have work to do," he said from behind her. "My home office is the library."

"Fine. Have at it," she replied as she mounted the staircase. "Though you might want to change."

Bryce glanced down at his clothes and silently groaned at the food splattered over him. He lifted his gaze to Ciara and his daughter stared at him over Ciara's shoulder. Bryce waved to his baby.

Carolina bounced up and down in Ciara's arms, kicking her feet, her cherub face lit up with happiness, as if to say, "See daddy, this is what it's like to have a mom."

Bryce's heart broke then and there.

And he decided he'd put up with just about anything to see his daughter smile like that. But how

would he survive with that luscious, mysterious
woman right under his nose? And regardless of what
he'd said, deep inside, in a place that was lonely and
hungry for female company, he wanted to experience
another mindless night of desire in Ciara's arms.

Ciara bathed Carolina, and dried her off before
warming baby lotion in her hands and rubbing it in
slow circular motions over the sleepy infant. The
child was nearly asleep on the changing table and
Ciara made quick work of putting on a diaper and
fresh clothes.

The infant fussed and rubbed her eyes, pulling at
her hair as Ciara sat in the padded rocker, humming
softly, the baby nuzzled on her chest. Ciara inhaled
the sweet scents, rubbing up and down Carolina's
spine, her own eyelids heavy with a comfort she
hadn't felt in a very long time. She thought and wondered then about her brothers and their children. She
hadn't seen her nephews in years and if her calcula-
tions were right, they were in school by now. Then
her thoughts drifted to her sister Cassie, who'd finished college summa cum laude and was off somewhere doing something that had nothing to do with
her financial degree. Ciara missed them all terribly.
She didn't usually, because she simply chose not to
think about them. It had become increasingly easy to
block out her past and her family, she thought with
regret. She'd never had time to sit back and think of
them, her mind had always been focused on her assignment. The cold objectivity was a part of her after
all these years. Her lips twisted with self-disgust. That
hadn't stopped her from letting old feelings darn near

ruin her career, she thought, and her anger at Mark Faraday settled like a simmering kettle in her chest. She left it there, refusing to waste more energy on him.

Her thoughts drifted immediately to Bryce.

She cocked a look at the sleeping baby in her arms, then stood and carried Carolina to her crib. Laying her down, she tried to remember if at this age they slept on their stomach or back, then laid Carolina on her tummy. Just before she did, Carolina opened her eyes, staring at her so trustingly, and Ciara thought suddenly that nothing she did in her life, nothing for her country, for the CIA, was more important than what she was doing right now. For this child. She stroked her back and the baby's eyes drifted closed.

How much tenderness had this little girl missed because she didn't have a mother? Bryce had to be both mother and father and Ciara remembered the different relationships she'd had with her parents. Her mom had been her role model, and made Ciara feel special, as if they shared a secret that men took years to understand. Ciara's mother had given her pretty things and taught her to take pride in her appearance for herself, not for anyone who might happen to notice. Ciara tried to pass that to Cassie. Yet her dad had been the one who let her hang with her brothers, who won the argument with her mother when she wanted to play soccer. Dad had kept telling her there was nothing she couldn't do. He'd pushed her to excel, to learn more than one language and make the grade to join the CIA.

Lord she missed them. But they were dead now, killed in a jet crash over Scotland. She hadn't been able to attend their funeral because she was stuck somewhere in Asia, hiding in a warehouse surveying gunrunners. And somehow, over the years, she'd lost the rest of her family, too. It was a hard fact to swallow, but Ciara admitted silently that though her parents were taken from her, she'd allowed her brothers and sister to fade from her life. Because of her career. Shame rippled through her along with a surprisingly sharp stab of homesickness.

The baby cooed in her sleep, wiggling under the thin blanket, and something hard wrenched in Ciara's chest. For some reason, she couldn't leave the baby just yet. Not alone. She was so little.

And for the first time in a long time, someone truly innocent, needed her.

Bryce stood in the doorway, studying Ciara. He tried not to notice how beautiful she looked there bent over his baby's crib, rubbing Carolina's back, watching her sleep. Seeing her there struck a chord in him and twisted his insides. She looked so at ease and though Carolina had known the touch of Bryce's mother and sister, it seemed that a perfect stranger was more soothing than either of them. Instantly he thought of Diana.

Would she approve?

Not if she knew he and Ciara had spent a night together. He'd never told anyone about that night, keeping it private, for himself alone. Telling Diana would have been mean and unnecessary. And caused more problems because she'd been possessive from the start, wanting him to quit the Secret Service for her and their unborn child. Married only a month, and seeing no way around it and feeling equally responsible, he had. Though he resented it at the time, and constantly being around her likely made things worse between them, he didn't resent leaving the service anymore. Not since his daughter had filled his life and his heart.

"She's so beautiful," Ciara said into the silence, startling him, and Bryce realized she'd known he was there all this time.

"Thank you." He watched her give the blankets a last tuck, then straighten and walk toward him. The tender look she gave his daughter still on her features.

He stared, absorbing it.

"How long have you been caring for her alone?"

"Other than when she was first born, a week."

"How do you get your work done?" she asked, admiration coloring her voice.

"I don't. I'm way behind. That's why I hired Wife Incorporated."

Ciara shoved her hands into the pockets of her jeans when she really wanted to touch him, run her hands over his taut muscled chest. "And here you get me."

Bryce saw the flicker of reservation in her eyes and wondered over it when she seemed so confident earlier. Trusting her seemed further away than he first thought. "Carolina seems to like you."

Ciara gazed up at him, her body sensing his, that current shooting up from her heels. "She's great."

Bryce experienced the same heady heat that drew him to Ciara that night in Hong Kong. She was inches from him, in the doorway and knowing he shouldn't, he lifted his hand to her face. Before he touched her, she stepped back, her tender expression vanished, replaced with an indifferent mask he already recognized.

His brow furrowed.

Her eyes were glacial, hard. Then she turned and walked down the hall.

Leaning on the door frame, Bryce watched her leave, thinking that no matter what they felt when they were near each other, there was a part of Ciara that was isolated, a woman hidden behind a wall. She might be gentle and tender with his daughter, but she wasn't letting down her guard.

Bryce went back to his office and remained there most of the day. With music playing in his office, he didn't hear any noise in the house and managed to catch up on the backlog of work. Yet when he glanced at his watch and realized how much time had passed and that he hadn't heard his daughter or Ciara in a while, he shot out of the chair and rushed to the door.

How could he be so careless? He knew nothing about this woman. And he'd left her and his baby alone together for hours.

Panicked, he stopped short in the hall, glancing left and right. "Ciara?" Thoughts of accidents filled his tired mind.

"Yes," she called from somewhere in the house. "In here."

Only a little relieved, he demanded, "Where the hell is here?"

"Well, duh, in the kitchen."

He nearly ran down the hall, his heart pounding and when he entered the room he froze. Carolina was tucked in her high chair, chasing cereal around her tray and stuffing as much as she could in her mouth, and Ciara was at the stove. For a second he just stared.

No one on this planet had a right to look that sexy in an apron.

And she'd changed into a tank top and cutoffs that had seen way better days, and were short as hell. They showed off every curve and for a moment, he let his gaze roam over her from head to bare toes. She moved efficiently, sautéing vegetables, checking something in the oven, then punching the timer on the microwave. Plus, glancing over at his daughter while she worked. It was as if she didn't know he was in the room now. And here he was, like a stag scenting a doe. The fact made him see how long it had been since he'd had a woman. A little over a year. He'd been married in name only, since he and Diana had wed when she was two months pregnant and they'd stopped sleeping together when her pregnancy became difficult, and that happened at the end of her first trimester.

Good grief, it had been a long time.

But then, he hadn't been interested in a woman until now.

And Ciara was the wrong one.

Shaking his head over his wildly racing thoughts, he went to his daughter, squatting to her level. "Did you have a nice nap, princess?"

Ciara glanced back over her shoulder smiling, trying to see only the father and not the man.

Carolina spit bubbles and offered him a Cheerio. He nibbled.

"How brave of you," Ciara said, focusing on chopping vegetables and tossing them in a pan. "Accepting food from that grubby little hand."

He kissed his daughter and straightened. "I'd do anything for her."

"I know. You're putting up with me for a nanny, aren't you?"

"I wouldn't have said it like that."

"But you were thinking it."

"Actually I was thinking that..."

She looked at him then, her brows drawn tight. "Go on, say it. We might as well be honest with each other from the start."

He wasn't going to mention that she was hiding damn near everything about herself from him already, and that was hardly honest. Instead he said, "I was thinking that you should put on more clothes."

Her features tightened. "Don't go there. Carolina and I were outside for a while and it's hot."

"Regardless, those," he gestured to the short shorts, "leave little to the imagination."

"Then force yourself to have *less* imagination, huh?" she said, pouring him a glass of tea, then placing it on the table before him.

"Kind of hard when I look at you and see you up against the wall, panting and wearing nothing but a strand of pearls."

Ciara's entire body clenched, her blood suddenly running very hot and fast.

She glanced his way briefly, flushing a little, and Bryce liked seeing it.

"That was a long time ago." She returned her attention to the meal she was cooking.

"You said yourself you were the same woman."

"I guess I lied."

"What else are you lying about?"

Her gaze snapped to his. "What the hell does that mean?" Don't get defensive, she warned herself. It will only add fuel to his suspicions.

"You're not being honest about your past."

She faced him and his gaze shifted to the knife in her hand. She put it down. "Want to open that door, Bryce? How about yours? Why did you leave the Secret Service?"

Old resentment reared. "I was tired of it."

"Oh yeah, the travel, great hotels, short work hours. A real pleasure killer."

"After I met my wife, yes." The half lie stuck in his throat like glue. He'd still be in the service right now if he hadn't met Diana.

Ciara felt unreasonably stung by that.

"And taking a bullet for someone who for the most part didn't know I was alive, didn't seem worth it after that." Not worth leaving his unborn baby without a father, he thought. "What about your family?"

Good lord, he wasn't getting the hint, was he? "I don't have one, anymore." In her line of work she'd had to cut all ties, yet for a second, the image of her brothers and her sister swept through her mind.

Bryce noticed the flash of pain in her eyes, the tightening of her features.

"You're alone, then."

"Yes." It wasn't a lie. She had to be alone. She couldn't contact anyone from her past and touching base with Katherine had been an operation in discretion and secrecy. "It's a choice thing. Don't sweat it."

"Does that mean you had some sort of falling out with family members?"

"You could say that." Or not. She wasn't giving him anything to chew on.

Good grief, Bryce thought, getting even a shred of information out of Ciara was like pulling teeth. He wondered if it had anything to do with why she was in Hong Kong. She had been an embassy secretary, she'd said. Bryce had his doubts. She hadn't acted like any secretary he knew and for a moment he remembered the lavish reception where he'd first seen her. Where he'd been stationed in one position, covering the doorways, she'd mingled with dignitaries, slipping around the ballroom, but there had been something... Was she with the NSA? CIA? FBI?

Ciara could see the cogs of his mind working for a solution. "Forget it Bryce, I'm not spilling my problems. Want a glass of wine with your dinner?" She walked to the cabinet to get it.

"Ciara, why are you so evasive?"

She spun around. "Why are you so interested in my past? It's nothing, average, and I don't want to relive it."

In the past thirty seconds, she decided to just make him believe that it was too horrible to remember. Then the images battered her: learning of her parents' death and taking over, taking Mom's place while her dreams were shelved for a while. Her brothers and their families and how much she missed being with them, and how much she couldn't. She'd always felt as if she were outside the fence, not allowed in, not allowed to experience love and tenderness. And a home. A real home. It hadn't bothered her. Well, not much. Not enough to do something about it, like leave the CIA, at least.

She lifted her gaze to Bryce's. Okay, so it hadn't bothered her until recently. But that didn't change a thing. It couldn't. Her career was all she had.

Yet Bryce and his baby girl touched her in places she'd been so certain were smothered. They were cracking through her training and she couldn't afford to let it happen. Regardless of the consequences to her and her heart, she had a job to return to and the sooner, the better.

Right now, Carolina needed her. Bryce didn't.

He was just being a man. He knew her in the biblical sense and felt that gave them a connection. It didn't. It wasn't deep, she told herself. It was just sex. Great sex, but one night didn't give them a past and she would make certain the coming weeks wouldn't, either. Yet the situation itself brewed intimacy. He was already too curious. She had to say and do the right things, keep her emotions and opinions under control. And not get near Bryce enough to want to touch him.

Because one stroke to her skin and it was as if she were a dried-up flower in need of the sweet touch of rain that only he could give her.

Three

―――

"I'll let it go for now," he said to her back. He could see that it hurt her to talk about her past.

Relief swept her and Ciara moved items on the counter uselessly.

"But not for long." He'd give his right arm to get a scrap of information out of her.

"I'm not important, Carolina is." Suddenly he was there, behind her, gripping her upper arms and Ciara closed her eyes and drank in the feeling. "Don't," she whispered. Oh mercy. *Nobody,* she thought, *nobody makes me feel like he does.* She couldn't get control of herself and almost twisted in his arms right then. "You've already made it clear I'm the help."

His lips were near her ear, his words sending a delicious chill down her throat. "You could never be."

She swallowed hard. "Bryce," she hissed softly,

the warm press of his body behind hers igniting fires that could never be extinguished.

"I had dreams about you saying my name like that. That night, with no names, no past or future. It was the most erotic one of my life."

Mine too, she thought, but wouldn't admit it. She was barely holding on to her control as it was.

Then he pulled her back against him, hard.

Bryce breathed in her scent, the feel of her this close, and though he knew he shouldn't, he pressed his mouth to her throat.

Her groan was low and wicked.

"Ciara. You're driving me nuts, you know."

"Same here." She kept her hands clenched tightly at her sides to keep from reaching back and touching him.

Then he slid his hands down her arms and around her waist, his palms splayed over her stomach and driving heat down to the core of her. "We have to forget about that night, Bryce. We have to or I can't stay here."

"It's hard to forget when I've kissed you, tasted you." He dragged his mouth down the side of her throat. "Been inside you," he said in a voice wrought with desire.

A sharp tingling spiraled out of control and, determined to hold tight to the resolutions she'd made only moments ago, Ciara twisted out of his arms.

"Don't."

Bryce simply stared as she turned off the range. Her hands were shaking. Hell, he was shaking. But with Ciara, this heat and fire, just...existed. No explanation. So how was he supposed to fight it?

Well, the way she was looking daggers at him

should help. But it didn't. It made him want to crack through that armor she threw up between them at will and find out why she did it.

Then Carolina squealed with delight.

And it was the smile she gave his daughter, warm and without hesitation, that softened him. But when she brought her gaze back to his, staring at him with cool indifference, Bryce wondered how she could turn her emotions on and off so easily. He sure as hell couldn't. And that reminded him that she'd strolled into his life one night like a hot summer storm and walked out just as easily without a backward glance.

Leaving him naked and hungry on a hotel room floor.

It hadn't bothered him then, but there was more at risk now. His daughter meant the world to him, and Bryce could see she was already attached to Ciara. He was grateful that if he couldn't be with his baby, at least Ciara was giving his daughter the attention she needed. And although he'd contracted for a permanent live-in nanny and housekeeper, she'd walked effortlessly away before. Would she do it again? Still, she wasn't here for his sake, he reminded himself as she bent to play with Carolina for a bit.

She was here for his daughter and he decided he wouldn't look for trouble so soon.

"Sit," Ciara said, pointing to the chair near Carolina.

Like a trained puppy he obeyed.

Ciara went back to the stove and served up the meal, placing the plate in front of him. Giving Carolina a glance to be certain she would be content for the next hour, Ciara surveyed the table, then walked toward the door.

"Where are you going?"

She paused at the doorway to glance back. "To my room."

He gestured to the seat at the table. "You're not joining me?"

"I'm the help, Bryce. And we need this line of division."

"The hell we do," he said and when her posture stiffened, her eyes hardening, he took another approach. "Come on, join me, it's boring eating alone. Carolina isn't exactly talking my ear off, you know."

Her gaze shifted to the child and he noticed how Ciara's expression softened.

"Come on."

Bryce left his chair and went to the cabinet, retrieving a plate, filling it, and setting it opposite his. He gathered utensils and when he plopped the last one down, he faced her.

If her expression could have gone colder, it did.

"No, Bryce. You aren't in the market more in this relationship and neither am I."

But it was tempting, so tempting. Especially when Carolina was working a Cheerio between her lips and bouncing up and down in her high chair. Her gaze shifted to Bryce, the table, then back to the child. It was as if she could forget her career and slip right into their lives. But she couldn't. She had a traitor to catch and a job to return to, hopefully, before she was gone too long and forgot what being a secret agent was all about.

She spun away and disappeared around the corner.

Bryce looked at his daughter, who had gone so far as to voice her opinion in a scream loud enough to peel wallpaper.

"I know, frustrating woman, isn't she?"

He dropped into his chair and picked up the fork. He didn't really see or taste the roasted pork loin stuffed with spinach and mushrooms. All he could envision was how cold Ciara could be when she wanted.

And right now, he thought, staring at the empty kitchen, she was knee-deep in ice.

After he'd finished his meal, Bryce cleaned the kitchen, stored the leftovers and flipped on the dishwasher. By then, Carolina was squirming to get out of the high chair and not making an effort to be dignified about it. Cleaning her off and lifting her into his arms, Bryce strolled around the house, telling himself that he was just looking around. He ended up alone in the sunroom, sinking down onto the flowered sofa, his daughter on his lap. She played with the buttons on his shirt and he studied his little girl, trying to see his late wife in his daughter's features and failing.

What would Diana think of her, he wondered, then knew. Diana had been possessive about him and she would be the same about their daughter. His late wife had seemed to be grasping for something, afraid he would be torn from her, and he supposed that came from her being orphaned at a young age and raised in the foster care system too long. But one thing was for sure, she would have loved her daughter with everything she had.

Slipping to the floor, he played with Carolina, watching her crawl across the carpet with amazing speed. Then he heard noise in the back part of the house and realized that Ciara was running a load of clothes through the washer. Just knowing she was closer, made his heart skip a little. And Carolina noticed, too. Her head lifted and she rolled around, her sharp gaze shooting to the doorway. She squawked, as if calling out and then patiently waited for an answer.

Bryce's gaze shot to the door and he, too, waited for Ciara to appear.

She didn't.

But her voice came to them. "It's bedtime for her, Bryce," she called. "Why don't you put her down for the night."

"No problem."

He enjoyed the nightly ritual. But realizing that Ciara wouldn't even face him, or come near to say good-night to Carolina, struck him like an arrow. He looked at his daughter, her expectant expression, and the same question plowed through his mind. If Ciara could turn away from him so easily, would she do that to his little girl?

Changing diapers and cleaning up after a baby was no comparison to some of the things Ciara had done in her career. Sitting on a wicker loveseat and watching a baby play in the grass, watching her explore her world, was sheer pleasure. The sun was warm, the breeze gentle and for once Ciara didn't have to watch her back. The house was isolated enough and riddled with a state-of-the-art alarm system. She could relax, for the first time in too long.

"No, sweetie, not in your mouth," Ciara said, lurching forward to remove grass from Carolina's tight fist. She gave her a spoon and shovel to bang and slid off the loveseat to join her little charge. She looked so much like Bryce it was uncanny.

Yet while she and the baby were getting along famously, Ciara and Bryce were not. He was at the office, the seafood company, working and had been for the past two days. He'd come home tired, eaten and then slipped back into his office to work some more, offering no explanation.

Not that she needed one.

But Carolina was missing her daddy.

It showed in the way she latched onto him when he leaned close to give her a kiss good-night. Ciara didn't have a problem with him being a workaholic. At least he trusted her with his daughter, she thought, glancing at the sun.

Deciding it was too hot for Carolina to be outside, she gathered up the child and strolled back toward the house. The pool looked too inviting to ignore and she stepped down the first step and sat on the tiled rim. Gently she scooped water over the baby's toes, letting her get used to the temperature. Then she dipped Carolina's toes into the cool water. She kicked and splashed, then when she realized all that noise and water was coming from her, she kicked wildly some more.

Ciara smiled, seeing the world through the infant's eyes. Like a bright shiny penny, and not a dull-edged cluster of loneliness.

She didn't see Bryce standing in the doorway several feet behind her.

He was silent as he watched them.

Carolina was cooing with pure delight when normally she screamed the instant he'd tried to put her feet in the water. Heck, he'd come to think that his daughter would be terrified of the pool for the rest of her life.

"Good girl!" Ciara said. "Pretty soon, you'll be dazzling us all with your swimming. You just wait, Carolina. Oh no, no diving," she said, gripping his daughter tighter when she wanted to sail headfirst into the water. "I think actually mastering freestyle would help first."

Carolina made noise, and Ciara laughed, hugging his baby close.

Slowly Bryce backed away and moved through the house and out the front door. He climbed into his car and slowly drove away. He'd come home to check on them, a little voice inside him telling him he shouldn't trust Ciara so easily. But when he'd seen them together, that was enough. Ciara might deny him, but he knew she'd never deny his daughter.

And somehow, that thought left him feeling cheated.

Ciara laid the baby down for her afternoon nap, gently unwinding her hair from Carolina's pudgy little fist. Carolina instantly shoved the fist into her mouth and curled on her tummy. Ciara covered her with a sweet-smelling blanket, then leaned over, resting her chin on the rail of the crib and just watching Carolina for a moment. Okay, she admitted, she loved the little southern belle. She hadn't wanted to, but this baby needed her so much.

But there was Bryce and the complication of him was just too much of a strain. Her insides felt twisted, her body alert and hungry, and her heart, well, that was bruised and wanting to be soothed. Something she couldn't indulge in right now. Being burned by Mark's infidelity was enough to scare her off relationships. Trusting men, especially one ex-Secret Service agent who sent her body into complete chaos, was not a good thing. Her survival training wasn't helping her much. She tried blocking the emotion, not giving Bryce an inkling that he could break her with just his touch. And she didn't know how long she could keep comparing Bryce with Mark and keep him out of her heart. She'd tried to see this as an assignment, an undercover masquerade, but it hadn't been like that, not even from the start. It fit too well.

It made her long for what she couldn't have. It made her more and more aware that he slept down the hall from her. She'd tasted his loving once, had experienced him with all the carnal pleasures a woman could want, and the knowledge made her feel like a high-strung thoroughbred champing at the bit.

If that evening in Hong Kong, those few hours were incredible, what would an entire night bring?

Stop, she mentally screamed at herself. *Sex isn't everything and he'd turn his back on you the instant he discovered you're CIA.*

It made her want to get out before either of them got hurt.

She knew Bryce thought avoidance was the answer, but for Ciara, just being on the same planet with that man was difficult. She had to leave. Now. Before it was too late. All she needed was one word from her supervisor about Mark Faraday that he'd been caught and she'd be off again, either testifying against Faraday as a witness to his crime or fulfilling a new assignment.

She left the nursery and went to her room. If Carolina could adapt easily to her, a stranger, she could do the same with anyone, right?

Ciara plopped onto the bed, and opened the mini

laptop, typing in the codes. Although she'd covered all the bases, disappeared without a trace as she'd done a hundred times before, there was that thread of risk to Carolina and Bryce she couldn't shake. She routed the computer phone line over the Internet and through four countries before she connected the phone to the computer and dialed. Ciara glanced at the door, then slid the small laptop under a pillow as a precaution. Katherine Davenport picked up instantly. They said hello, then Ciara got down to business.

"You need to replace me."

"What's wrong?"

"I can't do this to them."

"Honey, you have to talk to me more than that."

"It's him, Kat."

"Him? Who him?"

"Hong Kong," was all Ciara needed to supply.

"Oh Lordy, the one-night, no-name man of mystery you refused to give *me* any details about except a secret smile?"

Inwardly Ciara groaned. "Yes."

"Bryce Ashland was your one-night fling?" Apparently the one time she mentioned it after years of no contact—was coming back to gloat.

"Do I have to repeat myself? I know you're smarter than that."

"Oh, testy, huh?"

"You try to be around this man and see if he doesn't set your hormones jumping in five directions."

"Feeling vulnerable?" Sadistic pleasure rippled through those words.

"I can't afford to feel vulnerable," Ciara muttered.

It was all she could do not to go to Bryce and demand he make her feel like a woman again. Demand that he make love to her instead of just have wild sex. That very thought made her see how much trouble she was in already. Love was the last thing she needed now. In no more than three days of living in his house, of sleeping just down the hall from him, she was slipping out of her element. Too quickly. And she was afraid she'd never get back to her career. And she wanted to be back, if anything to see her former partner Mark Faraday go down for his betrayal.

"I can't stay here," she said, trying to convince herself as well as Kat. "His daughter is too adorable and she deserves someone better than me. Someone who'll stick around. Someone who can really be a mother to her. You have to get me out of this. I have to leave."

"I guess I can find—" Kat started to say.

The phone was snatched from Ciara's hand.

Her head jerked up and she found Bryce hovering over her.

"No," he said into the receiver.

Jumping to her feet, Ciara reached for the phone. "Bryce! This is a private conversation."

"Too bad. I heard."

He kept the phone from her and Ciara had the urge to take him to the ground like one of the hundreds of suspects she'd left incapacitated in the past. But that would reveal the secret she needed to keep.

He put the phone to his ear. "She's not leaving, so whoever this is, forget it."

"This is Katherine Davenport and Ciara feels the need to leave and was calling for a replacement."

"I don't need one and we have a contract."

Katherine's voice sharpened. "You have one with my company, Mr. Ashland, not with my employee."

Bryce felt cornered. "She's not leaving." He shut off the phone and tossed it on the bed.

Ciara contained her temper for all of two seconds, then with a low growl, she planted her hands on his chest and shoved. "How dare you! That was my private call. It was none of your business!" She advanced until she was in his face, full of fury.

"It is, if it concerns my daughter."

"Liar! This has nothing to do with Carolina." She jabbed a finger at his chest. "This is you invading *my* privacy. Dammit, Bryce. I thought I could at least trust you this far."

"Trust? You have more secrets than the U.S. government."

Bryce gazed down at her, accepting the full brunt of her fury.

"I'm outta here," Ciara snapped.

Before she could move, he grabbed her up against him, his mouth descending on her with the muttered words, "The hell you are."

Four

Any retort Ciara had was cut off, blunted by his mouth crushing over hers. He put everything he had into the kiss, using the strength of his desire and her weakness for him. And it worked.

She came unglued, slapping her arms around his neck, driving her fingers into his hair.

Damn.

It was the same.

Only stronger. Harder.

Passion erupted between them in a powerful wave and Ciara was helpless as it swept over her, shutting everything else out and filling the loneliness that had been her only company for so many years. She surrendered to it. Her hands roamed over his chest, her fingers flipping open his shirt buttons, then diving inside. He moaned at her first touch, trembled as her fingers met flesh.

His kiss grew harder, devouring, and when he pushed his hand under her shirt and discovered she was naked, he thought his knees would cave.

"Oh Ciara," he groaned softly as he filled his palms with her breasts, his thumbs circling her nipples and she thrust into him, almost climbing up his body.

Bryce lifted her and her legs wrapped his hips. He shoved her top up and took her nipple deep inside his mouth. She cried out softly, throwing her head back, holding him there as he laved and nipped, suckled harder until she thought her insides would shatter.

"Sweet mercy Bryce, it's the same," she whispered.

"No, no," he managed over his rough breathing. "Better." He staggered back, then sank to the floor, not giving her a moment to think, only to feel, his mouth on her skin, his hands molding over her body.

Straddling his thighs, she kissed him with a ferocity that left him moaning, his hands rushing over her as if to touch every inch in one sweep, then try again. She was no less busy, shoving his jacket off, peeling open his shirt, stroking down between his legs and shaping his arousal. He made a dark hungry sound, like the rumbling of a storm, and gripped her hips, thrusting against her in the dance they'd once shared.

Ciara gasped and answered him with a hard push, wanting to feel him inside her. His mouth was on her breast again, his fingertips diving below the waistband of her slacks, then sweeping around to the zipper. He sent it down and pushed beneath the fabric, her panties, fingers sliding lower, seeking her wet warmth, and the instant his touch neared her center, she knew she couldn't do this.

She stilled and he immediately noticed it.

He lifted his head and knew this would go no further.

"I can't do this."

"You were doing right nicely a second ago."

She pushed off his lap and righted her clothing as she said, "This was why I was leaving. I can't live here and do this with you." She stood.

"You want me."

She choked off a short laugh. "I don't think there is any doubt."

"I want you like mad."

She looked at him. The tender smile she sent him was so unrestricted, so free, his heart skipped and crashed in his chest. He wanted to see that look all the time.

"I know. But..."

"But what?" he said as he stood.

"I can't look at you in the morning and know that we have only this between us."

He rubbed his face, still breathing hard. She was right. He didn't like that he wanted more. He didn't like that he wanted *more* so badly.

Her voice came soft, and almost distant as she said, "We used each other that night in Hong Kong, Bryce. We both knew it. That's why I said no names and you agreed. If I'd wanted more—"

"I know," he interrupted, meeting her gaze. "You would have looked me up. But did you ever think of what I wanted then?" He'd torn up the city looking for her the next day.

"No, I couldn't. I still can't."

"Why?" What the hell was she hiding?

"I have my reasons. And you already made it clear that you're not looking for a wife, so that leaves easy companionship. Well, no dice. Sleeping with you while I'm your daughter's nanny just makes me feel cheap."

"Don't say things like that."

"Well, that's how I see it. We used each other five years ago. And that was fine with me. Then. Not now." Not when I know your name, not when I see you like a man and not a fantasy, she thought, swallowing hard. "I'll be gone in the morning." She turned to the closet and pulled out her suitcases.

"What about Carolina?"

"She's a good baby. She'll take to anyone." Ciara opened dresser drawers, walking woodenly to and from the suitcase. "Wife Incorporated will send someone to replace me."

Bryce stood there, still reeling from their kiss and she was like this cool efficient machine. Cutting him out before she split.

Without a doubt in his mind he knew if she left, he'd never see her again.

She'd gotten to him. Five years ago and five seconds ago. And he knew he was about to make a fool of himself for a woman who didn't want him.

"Well, there is a problem," he said, yet she kept packing. "Just anyone won't do and the last nanny neglected Carolina."

Ciara turned from where she was tossing her things into a suitcase. "What do you mean?"

"I came home unexpectedly and Carolina was in her playpen, crying, wet, dirty and hungry. And from the look of it, she'd been that way for hours. God knows what else the woman did to her.''

Instant fury filled Ciara, the mere thought of anyone neglecting a child making her see red. ''Did she have marks on her?'' Her voice snapped with anger.

''No, thank God.''

''Did you bring charges?''

''With what evidence? Yes, I fired her, called the agency and tried new ones. But Carolina screamed her head off any time a stranger came close to her.''

Ciara's brows knitted and she thought of the little baby sleeping down the hall, of anyone scaring her. ''But she didn't with me?''

''My point exactly.''

''Oh, that's unfair, Bryce.''

He knew that. And inside, he refused to admit that he wanted Ciara to stay for more than because his daughter was comfortable with her.

''You can find someone else,'' she said and turned her back on him. She couldn't stay. She'd already sunk too deep and though she had no idea where she'd go, where she'd hide 'til Faraday was caught, she knew she couldn't take being near Bryce when she wanted him so badly.

''I don't have time,'' Bryce said. ''I've got negotiations for a deal that will set my company for life, not to mention the mountain of paperwork piling up at the office. I can't work and search for a new nanny at the same time. And I don't want to be forced to take the next nanny that applies. Not after last time.''

Ciara's shoulders sank. He was wearing her down and she realized her survival skills were useless around Bryce Ashland.

"Look Ciara, if you can stand being near me, stay for Carolina's sake."

Ciara forced herself to fold and lay her clothes into the case. "Cheap shot."

"I'm desperate." Bryce felt as if he was losing a battle he wasn't sure he wanted to win.

She faced him, her gaze clashing with his.

Damn, Bryce thought. He hated that frosty stare. And it hurt to see it aimed at him. It was as if Ciara could take her heart out and put it on a shelf 'til she needed it.

"Okay, I'll stay."

Shock and relief swept through him and made his shoulders droop.

"But under one condition."

Figures, he thought. "What?"

"No touching me." She was just too vulnerable when it came to him.

"Agreed."

She eyed him suspiciously, in a way that made him see the woman in Hong Kong who'd easily left him on the hotel room floor.

"Okay, we have a deal—"

Suddenly Carolina cried out, and without a glance, Ciara left the room, racing to his child.

She might put her heart on a shelf where he was concerned, but with this baby, she wore it on her sleeve. He glanced at her suitcase, then left the bedroom, wondering why he just didn't leave it alone. It wasn't bad enough that he'd destroyed Diana's life, what would he do to Ciara's if given the chance?

A chance she wasn't allowing. Probably a good thing, he thought. One night years ago left a mark on them and although it fed memory and desire, there wasn't anything there for a future. Not that he wanted one. And she sure as hell had made it clear she didn't.

Great sex just wasn't enough anymore.

At least, not for him.

Three days later, in the darkened house, Ciara slipped out the French doors and walked quickly to the gazebo. Sitting down on the curved bench, she instantly opened the small laptop, stretched her fingers and started typing. A familiar excitement raced through her as she watched the screen, routing her phone line through a hotel in Switzerland, an airport in Australia, one in Tokyo and a half dozen other places before ending at her unit at the CIA. The Intel computer phone rang and Ciara, opting for the headset instead of the phone, put it on just as it rang on her senior supervisor's desk. He was the only person she could trust.

"Patterson."

"Indigo Alpha, 4-0-8," Ciara said and heard the appropriate clicks that scrambled the line.

"How you doing, kid?"

Only her boss would call a thirty-year-old agent a kid. "Fine. Any light in the tunnel?"

"No, lay low. He's still free. It's going to take some time. I'll contact you."

Her first instinct was that he was in on it with Faraday and trying to get a location out of her. Just to be sure, she covered her bases. "You can't. I'm as deep under as it gets," she said with a glance at the plush yard and grand house.

She was trained mostly in surveillance, and sure as

hell knew more about satellite positioning, weapons, terrorist factions and Intel, than she did about keeping house and chasing after a baby. And avoiding contact with Bryce. He'd been good about keeping his promise of not touching her. In fact, he'd taken it so far as to not look at her most of the time. Their relationship was strictly professional. He'd turned into a complete workaholic and for the past three days she'd left his dinner in the microwave with a note. And other than seeing him briefly in the morning before he left for the office, they'd had little contact. And she silently admitted she missed him. No matter how much she didn't want to.

"You there?"

She blinked and shook her thoughts loose of Bryce. "I sent you a souvenir."

"Oh yeah? Is it socks? I need socks."

She smiled to herself, glad that the carefully worded letter was on its way to him while at the same time the videotape of Mark Faraday betraying his country and colleagues was out of her hands and now meandering across the country through varied post offices to a neutral party. That way, all bases were covered—if the tape didn't come out, the neutral party would go looking for it. "Better than argyles," she said. "I'll check in later. It's not going to hurt my career to miss a few days of work, right boss?"

His chuckle was computerized as it came through the headset, but in her mind she replaced it with the rich baritone she knew well.

"Getting antsy already. Figures."

"I'm outta here," she said, then cut the line in Australia first. She couldn't leave a trail to this house, these people. She was the one who took the risks for her country, not them. Closing up, and pushing the small thin computer into her case, she zipped it closed, then headed back to the house. She quietly opened the doors and slipped inside, moving quickly through the house to the staircase.

She froze when a shadow rose in front of her and instinctively she reached for the weapon that wasn't there.

"So Ciara," Bryce said, folding his arms over his chest. "Are you going to tell me why you were out in the backyard at midnight?" He flicked on the hall light and his gaze dropped to the case in her hand. "With that?"

Ciara's spine stiffened.

Bryce's first thought was that she was just out for a stroll. Then he saw the bulge in the case that could only be a phone.

And his next thought was she was calling a man.

And jealousy tore through him. Especially when he noticed how she was dressed.

Or rather *not* dressed.

The short nightgown and thin robe left little to his imagination. And where she was concerned, his imagination had the speed of sonic flight. And the sexy deep burgundy satin molding her body sent his own desires into overdrive. He grew hard, instantly. He imagined her with another man, any man, giving him all that lush passion Bryce had known so long ago, and something tightened around Bryce's chest like a vise.

Then the talk he'd had with himself earlier kicked in and he tried smothering his runaway passion. Suddenly he resented the hell out of the things Ciara did to him. Making him think of more, making him want more than he wanted to consider, even in a private fantasy. One look at her and he thought of being inside her, feeling her arch against him and of the satisfaction he'd felt with her, and only her. And in a small secret part of his mind, a place even he dared not go too often, he realized that not even his wife had made him feel that way.

Wild sex with a stranger had.

What did that say about his ability to choose a mate? And was he fantasizing about that because that's all they'd had? Mentally he shook himself free of those thoughts.

"Well," he finally said. "What is that?"

"My computer."

It was incredibly small, he thought and he didn't think he'd ever seen one so thin. And then there was the phone. "What are you doing with it outside?"

"Using it."

Damn her evasiveness. "For what?"

"I don't think that's any of your business."

She started past him, but he latched onto her arm.

"Let go."

He didn't. "You were outside in the pitch black, using a computer? With a phone?"

"Yes. And the phone is for Internet links." She searched his gaze. "What's your problem?"

"Believing you."

Ciara sighed hard and knew this would only bring an argument she didn't want or need. She pulled free and faced him. "It's a lovely night, the screen is lit enough that I can see it and I wanted to be outside."

Bryce's gaze thinned. He still didn't believe her. But he'd be damned if he'd admit he was jealous.

"What are *you* doing up? Spying on me?"

"No, I couldn't sleep." *Because you're three doors down the hall,* he thought.

"Then go to work. Maybe it will give you some free time with Carolina later."

He scowled, resentment riding his spine. "Don't change the subject. My daughter has nothing to do with you lurking outside at midnight."

"I don't lurk. Do you want to see the computer, look at its history?" She held out the computer, glad that she routinely cleared the login history.

Bryce's gaze shifted to the case, then to her. It was a challenge. Then again everything with her felt like a challenge. And why was he acting like a jealous lover when he didn't want a relationship with her, with any woman? He'd no right to question what she did on her off time. "No."

Ciara let her arm drop to her side. "Good, because Carolina is the only reason I'm in this house, Bryce."

Although the dig stung, he suddenly smiled.

She frowned. "What?"

"You're a sucker for babies, aren't you?"

Her lips curved and she shook her head, laughing to herself. Grateful for the change of subject, she said, "Yeah, who'd have thought, huh?"

His suspicions fading, he said softly, "Not me."

Ciara felt his gaze slide up and down her body, making her feel half-clothed. She sent him a warning look.

He ignored it. "I know Carolina misses me, and

I'd love to stay home all day, but I can't. I've almost closed this deal. When I do, then there will be time.''

Then I'll be gone, she thought, and the knowledge bit through her heart. She'd be here only until Mark was caught and it was safe to come out of hiding. What had she gotten herself into here? She was nuts about a little baby girl and more than a little crazy about the baby's daddy. Heck, maybe she was just plain crazy, because this was more involvement than she ever intended.

"How about some wine? Will that help you sleep?"

Boy, she shifted like the wind. "Sure."

She set the computer case by the stairs and turned back into the kitchen. Each step made her suddenly aware of how she was dressed. Ah, well, he's seen me in less, she thought, then crushed back the thought as she went to the cabinet and retrieved a wine bottle. He stopped beside her, taking it and using the corkscrew to open it. She got out the glasses, setting them on the counter and covertly watching him. In drawstring pajama slacks and a robe, he looked so sexy. The robe was paisley gray, open and showing the smooth lean muscle of his chest and stomach. Washboards, she thought and wondered when he had the time to stay in shape like that.

And her fingers started to itch.

Like they had when she'd seen him in Hong Kong, across the banquet room in that black suit, his gaze constantly scanning the crowd for the unknown assailant ready to attack the former first lady.

He didn't look much different to her now. Well, clotheswise, but like then, she'd seen beneath them.

Bryce poured and held out the glass to her. "Ciara?"

She blinked and accepted it, yet said, "I don't have trouble sleeping." She'd lived for years on less than four hours sleep a night.

"Clear conscience?"

"Guilty one?" she retorted.

He smirked. "Nope. Pure as the driven snow."

His thoughts exploded with the images of Diana and guilt washed over him in hard waves.

His expression tightened. He gulped his drink, staring somewhere near the edge of the counter and wishing the wine would wash away the image of her dying to give birth to the child she wanted from a man who didn't love her.

At that moment, he couldn't remember any good times and that hurt as much as the guilt. He could scarcely recall Diana's smile, what it felt like to hold her. What he felt when he did. She wasn't gone even a year.

What kind of man did that make him?

An undeserving one, he thought and lifted his gaze to Ciara.

Five

Ciara frowned, wondering what hole he just fell into. His expression looked pained and distant and she replayed that last bit of conversation.

A guilty conscience? This Boy Scout? And over what?

"That look is making me curious," she said.

Bryce blinked. "Turnabout is fair play, I guess."

He was hiding secrets too, Ciara thought. "You never play fair, Ashland."

His sudden smile was devastating, and although she felt it was a little forced, when he inclined his head to the sunroom, she went like a trained puppy. Pathetic, she thought and wondered if she was just hungry for male company. With a male who wasn't trying to get national secrets out of her.

He settled into the big overstuffed chair.

Ciara thought he looked odd against the flowery pattern as she found her now favorite spot near the window. She curled up into the corner of the sofa and gazed out the window. The moonlight splashed across the water and the shore. It looked like glass, and she let out a soft sigh. This was truly a heavenly place. And if things were different, she might have been able to dream about staying here. Belonging. A soft smile crossed her lips at the ridiculous yearning.

Bryce sipped his wine, watching her. The robe had slipped off her shoulder, her hair spilling down her back in long chestnut curls. He said what was on his mind.

"You're beautiful, Ciara."

Her lips curved gently, yet she kept staring out the window. "Thank you." It had been a long time since she'd heard that. From any man. And from this one, it was dangerous. She changed the subject instantly. "You're lucky. This is an incredible place."

He studied her, her chin in her palm, her elbow braced on the back of the sofa. She looked serene and content. Almost as if it were the first time in her life she'd relaxed.

"Well, you're easily amused I see."

She smiled and kept staring. "Simple pleasures," she said softly as if talking too loud would destroy them.

"I loved growing up here. It has everything anyone could want. I wish I could spend more time enjoying those simple pleasures."

"Me, too."

He knew she meant with Carolina.

"I'd forgotten what they were," she said.

"How so?"

"No real chance to enjoy them, I guess."

"Well this is a small town with a lot of simplicity. It's home. Safe and a good place to raise Carolina." He paused and then said, "It's not exactly Hong Kong though, is it?"

Okay, she thought, that zinger didn't hit too hard. "Why did you leave the Secret Service?"

"My wife needed me home." Bryce frowned slightly. He'd never said that out loud to anyone. He'd made excuses to himself and Diana about leaving the Secret Service two months after they married, that he was tired of the traveling, of the risks. But that wasn't it. He'd felt responsible for her happiness. Or rather, her lack of it. He couldn't love her and had ruined her life. It was that simple and that difficult to forget.

"She didn't like you traveling, huh?"

"Diana wasn't good at being alone and…I'd rather not talk about her." *Not to you,* he thought. Hell, not to anyone.

Ciara nodded, understanding his late wife's situation. It's the reason she'd never married, and why most of her fellow field agents were single or divorced. They were never home when they were needed and wives and husbands who couldn't handle the secretiveness and long absences usually strayed or left altogether.

Oh, what we do for our country, she thought, then watched a gull swoop down to the water to pluck a fish from the sea. It made her breath catch.

"What is it?"

"A gull. Night fishing."

He rose and moved closer to her, peering out the window. "It's a hawk."

She looked up. In that instant she appeared innocent and a little scared. He eased to the sofa beside her and set his wineglass on the coffee table. He pointed to the long dock. "I've had that little johnboat since I was sixteen," he said, gesturing to the battered craft beside the cabin cruiser. "There isn't a part of these rivers that I don't know."

"When was the last time you were out there?"

He sighed to himself. "Too long to think about."

"Maybe you need to do it again. Of course, the cabin cruiser would be more comfortable."

Her dry tone didn't escape him. "Yeah, but seeing the river from a little boat like that, it's just better all around, more in touch with the wildlife. Wild hogs come down to the shore, you know."

She didn't, but that was hardly on her mind right now. His attention was focused on her and he reached, touching her hair, sweeping it off her neck.

Instantly she tensed and eyed him, pulling the robe up over her shoulder. "Trying to seduce me, Bryce?"

"Will it work?"

Yes, oh yes, she thought. "Sure."

His muscles clamped hard at that.

"But that's not what you want."

He frowned. "How can you be sure?"

"I can't, but you could have any woman you wanted. I may be convenient, but I'm not the forever type."

"Who said I wanted forever?"

"We've been down this road, remember? Yesterday. Or was it the day before?"

"Or five years before."

Her lips thinned. "You really need to let that go."

She was more than right, yet something in him, something he didn't understand pushed him on. "I keep seeing you—"

"Don't."

"Feeling you."

"Bryce. Quit that." She left the couch, setting her glass down as she did.

Absently he realized she hadn't drunk any of it.

"Running again, Ciara?"

"I'm staying here for Carolina. So that means you stay away."

"I'm trying, God knows I am. But I have this almost uncontrollable need to touch you."

"Well stuff it somewhere! I won't be used again!"

He scowled. Did she mean like they'd used each other in Hong Kong, or by someone else?

"You don't want me, Bryce, trust me. One night was all we had or ever will. I couldn't give more than that if I wanted."

He eyed her thoughtfully. "Why do I believe you now?"

"Because it's true." She paused and then said, "We have nowhere to go, understand?"

He didn't say anything as he stood. She backstepped and hated the cowardly move.

But this man had an arsenal all his own. He had weapons that had first-strike capability. His eyes. Oh, he had the sexiest eyes. That sly stare that spoke volumes and made her feel incredibly exotic when she was just average.

And now he was wasting that charisma on her. She

couldn't, would not let herself fall any deeper. Though she desperately wanted to take what that velvety look promised.

Bryce advanced, stopping inches from her. "Keeping our distance hasn't been easy so far."

She laughed shortly. "Tell me about it."

"And if you'd quit looking at me like that, it might help."

Ciara's brows knitted slightly. "Looking what way?"

"Like you want me to strip you down right now."

Oh, she did, she thought. She really did. Then she lied, "You're reading what you want to see." She *really* had to get better control over herself, she thought.

He shook his head slowly. "If there is one thing I know about you, Ciara, it's what you look like when you want me."

How had she become so transparent when it was her job not to be? "Keep thinking of me as the nanny, and that should help."

"Okay. And I'll be the boss."

"Boss, no, employer, yes."

He laid his hands on her shoulders and her heart skipped and dove in her chest.

"You have to stop touching me. You agreed."

"One last time," he whispered.

"No." There was a plea in her tone no one could mistake.

"Yes."

His mouth neared.

Ciara knew she was lost. Just looking into his eyes, she came unwound, like silk ribbons refusing to stay neatly tied. Then his mouth touched hers and her insides liquefied, and she swore her willpower slithered to the floor to puddle at her feet.

His arms came around her. Slowly this time, meandering. His kiss was gentler, more controlled, but greedy. With exquisite patience, he worried her lips and her toes curled in the carpet. He swept his tongue across her lips and her body gravitated toward him. Slowly he pressed her to his length and she felt every strong inch of him imprinting to her body.

This was unfair. This was different.

This wasn't the out-of-control passion.

It was seduction. Slow deliberation. His tongue pushed between her lips and she moaned darkly, wrapping her arms around his waist and pulling him harder to her. His breathing was as fast as hers, escalating with each passing moment. Emotion poured through this kiss when before, it was simply raw, blinding passion. It made her heart clench.

Her hands pushed up his back, feeling his strength and wanting to lean into it. On it. To be safe and wanted. His mouth rolled erotically back and forth over hers, each stroke, each pass uncoiling the passion she'd tried to suppress. It was sweet and heady like the fragrance of magnolias in the early summer. Lingering and poignant. Wrapping her comfortingly. It was one last time before the defenses went up, she told herself, before she had to say no to her emotions. She opened wide for him, seizing the moment for herself. For later, when she was alone again. When she was longing for things she couldn't have, for a real life. For normalcy. For a life with him and his daughter.

That thought rocked her to her heels.

Ciara tore her mouth from his, then quickly pushed out of his arms.

She touched her mouth for a moment, then her wildly beating heart as she lifted her gaze to his.

Bryce saw the sheen of tears in her dark eyes.

"Don't *ever* do that again," she whispered hotly before she turned and fled from the room.

He knew what she meant. Don't kiss her like he meant it. Don't hold her like he never wanted to let go.

He'd felt it, too. The difference. The change in himself and in her. It had only been a moment, but it was enough. And it shook him to his soul. That kiss had only made this worse. He hadn't meant to show her that. Ever. Yet he hadn't gotten her out of his system five years ago and he hadn't now.

She was in his blood.

And just short of dying, he wondered how they were going to keep on living together.

Bryce got what he deserved, he supposed. Ciara was ice-cold toward him the next morning, hardly sparing him a glance as she tended to his daughter. It was as if he'd breached an unknown line in her defenses and those walls were right back where they'd started. The door was closed.

No one was allowed in.

It stung, since he'd barely slept last night thinking about it.

And if the dark circles under her eyes were any indication, she'd been thinking about it, too.

"Come on, sweetheart, let's get you all dolled up

for public viewing,'' she told Carolina as she lifted her out of her high chair.

''Public viewing?'' Bryce said, taking a last sip of coffee before he had to leave.

''We're going to the park.''

''Be sure to put some sunscreen on her, it gets...''

''I have it covered,'' Ciara said in a monotone as she pried little baby fingers from her hair.

''I imagine you do.''

Her gaze snapped to his. The silence between them pulsed and Bryce said, ''Ciara, about last night...''

''No. No more last nights or five years ago or anything, Bryce. No nothing but Carolina.'' She propped the baby on her hip. ''How much clearer do I have to be?''

She didn't expect an answer, but she couldn't keep her distance emotionally if he kept bringing up their sexual attraction for each other. It was that kiss last night, like no other before, and sometime during the night Ciara admitted it had scared the hell out of her, made her feel stripped and vulnerable and weak. Because she'd wanted more. She wanted to slip easily into a role she'd no business considering.

She was temporary.

Very temporary.

She was a CIA agent, surveillance specialist, covert operation. She was good at what she did. She even had an alias, a code name, and heck, Stuart wasn't even her real last name.

If Bryce knew any of that, she'd be out of here as fast as last week's trash.

She'd been right about him. He was deadly, a foe that was too hard to fight. Especially when he kissed her like he…like he adored her. Like he wanted more from her than to rekindle a long ago night. And she didn't know what she *wasn't* willing to risk more. His anger, or losing these few days of being normal. Of just being Ciara. Mentally she snickered at her own audacity. She was lying to him, what was normal about that?

At her bitter expression, Bryce's brows drew down, his scowl as hard as hers. He wondered what was going on in that sharp mind, besides drawing more barriers. He'd known something had changed between them last night, in that single kiss. It had suddenly involved deeper emotions. It spoke of a gamble she didn't want any part of, and neither did he. He reminded himself that he'd already screwed up one woman's life, and likely would again if he kept at it long enough.

He stood, reaching for his jacket. "I'll be late," he said, slipping it on.

With a sharp nod, she left the kitchen and he followed. They parted in the foyer, yet a whine came from his daughter and Carolina, not to be denied, pouted at her father's inattention. Bryce smiled gently and stepped close, running his hand over his baby's downy curls and kissing her. "Bye, my princess," he whispered and then lifted his gaze to Ciara's.

Frosty eyes stared back at him, yet her hand lovingly stroked his daughter's back. If ever there was a fortress, he thought.

"See you later," she said, then turned and mounted the stairs, still smelling his cologne and still feeling the heat of his body that her knees almost folded. Damn him, she thought.

Bryce walked to the door. He was halfway out when something made him stop. He glanced back over his shoulder, unwilling to admit he needed a last look at her. While cool tension radiated from her like a winter chill, even with her back to him, Carolina was happily gurgling away in her arms, completely unaware of the trouble between them.

Bryce wondered for the hundredth time why he could give himself a good talking to about why he shouldn't get involved, in any form, and be prepared to face Ciara down, then take one look at her, and all the warnings vanished.

He admitted she was a weakness he never knew he had.

And one he planned to fight. Big talk, he thought as he stepped outside and closed the door behind him. His life with Diana was a harsh reminder of the pain he could cause. And even as cool a customer as Ciara was, he couldn't do that to her.

"Ciara, look who wants to join in."

Ciara looked up from teaching three children to swim, to where Bryce's sister, Hope, was sitting under the shade of the deck overhang. Hope pointed to Carolina, who had one chubby leg hiked up in a feeble attempt to climb out of the playpen.

Ciara smiled. "My lord, she hasn't even taken her first steps and already she wants to run." Making the kids sit on the side of the pool, she went to the baby, gently pushing her leg down and telling her no.

Carolina's lower lip curled down.

"Don't try that pout with me, young lady," Ciara said. "This is for your own safety." Carolina dropped down onto her diaper-padded rump and whimpered. Fat tears filled her blue eyes. Ciara took pity and lifted her out of the playpen.

"Wimp," Hope said laughingly as she traded places with Ciara as lifeguard.

Ciara knew there was a guilty look smeared over her face, but she just couldn't stand to see her little charge unhappy when she kept thinking about that other nanny neglecting her. She didn't want Carolina to think she was the same. At that thought, she smirked to herself, wondering if the child thought of her as anything but the person who kept her dry and well fed.

Settling in a lounge chair, she watched the children and three mothers playing in the pool. She'd met Bryce's sister Hope at the park when Hope recognized Carolina, and Ciara had struck up an easy conversation with the dark-haired woman, which surprised her, since she hadn't had much chance to talk to any woman who wasn't an agent, or a source. Ciara never expected the quick friendship forming with these women, she admitted. She'd little in common with Hope or her two friends, Portia and Katey.

That reality had hit her when she was driving over to the park and found herself looking for snipers, escape routes and possible threats. It had taken a few minutes to remember where she was. She'd bet a year's pay that not another woman at the park, or in this town had done *that* this week. She reminded herself that she wasn't in danger, that her only real care in the world was making Bryce's baby happy. She wasn't used to it and wondered if she could ever forget her past and be normal.

Because pathetically normal sounded so damned appealing lately.

When the morning grew increasingly hotter, Ciara had suggested to Hope and the other women that they come over to use the pool. The moms snapped at the chance. Apparently, Hope hadn't been over in a while because her brother hadn't invited her. Something Ciara found appalling.

And made her suspect that Bryce was still mourning his late wife.

But then, Ciara had family she hadn't seen in years, so who was she to criticize?

Suddenly, Hope plopped down beside her and smiled brightly. "So, how's life with my big brother?" she asked cheerily.

Ciara had wondered when they were going to get around to the personal stuff. They'd been polite and friendly, but she could tell the women were itching to ask about Bryce. "Interesting."

Hope smiled knowingly. "Yeah, I'll just bet. I did notice he's been at work a lot lately. Some late hours."

"He's catching up on overdue work, I imagine." And avoiding me.

"Baloney," Portia said from the pool, her infant son propped on her hip. "He's hiding from life. He can afford to have some shorter days."

"Yeah, he never goes out, rarely shows up at family outings unless I holler real loud," Hope said. "I think that's why mom and dad moved to Florida. They got tired of his refusals."

"He did lose his wife." Why was Ciara defending

him? From what she'd learned, he'd been a hermit and had kept his daughter secluded with him.

"I know. But he wasn't much different before Diana came into the picture. He took the Secret Service stuff way too seriously."

"It's a serious job." What would they think of hers?

"I still think he resents that he had to leave it."

"Had to?" Ciara said and tried not to sound too surprised.

"Diana wanted him home more."

"He must have loved her a lot to give up the Secret Service."

The other women exchanged an odd look.

"Or not," Katey muttered half under her breath.

Ciara smoothed the baby's hair. Curiosity was killing her, but she wasn't going to pry. She didn't have to.

Hope said, "Diana and Bryce knew each other briefly, as in one night."

So did I, Ciara thought, yet he married Diana. Not liking the train of her thoughts or wanting to hear any more about Bryce and his late wife, Ciara rose. "I need to feed Carolina. How about I make some lunch for all of us?"

The other women exchanged a sly look she didn't see.

"We brought lunch." Hope pointed to the thermal coolers they'd dragged in with the eager children. "We were going to have it at the park. Though this is way better."

"Yeah, swimming will tucker them out and maybe give me some fun time alone with that man I married,'' Katey said, wiggling her brows as she climbed out of the pool. She fetched the coolers, while Portia, with her son in her arms, grabbed a diaper bag and tossed it on the table. Ciara watched her maneuver on the most amazing instinct; shoving her hand into the diaper bag and coming back with a diaper, wipes and a bottle. With the fussing child against her shoulder, Portia managed to open a drink for her older son, lay out his lunch, wipe his mouth, feed her infant son and change him, all the while chatting easily with everyone.

Amazing.

Ciara put Carolina in the playpen so she could prepare her lunch. When she came back with Carolina's high chair, she noticed the others staring at her.

''What? Is my butt hanging out of my suit?'' she said, snapping the elastic lower over her behind.

Then she noticed they were staring *past* her.

On instinct, Ciara brought the high chair up in front of her in a defensive move as she spun about. The legs of the chair hit a solid wall of man and sent him stumbling sideways toward the pool.

Ciara watched in horror as Bryce, in a tailored business suit, flailed wildly to keep from falling in the water.

Six

Ciara instantly dropped the high chair and reached for him.

With a helpless, wide-eyed look, he caught her hand, and fought for balance...and lost. The force of his weight and the simple tug of gravity sent them both into the pool.

Under the shallow water, Ciara fell hard against him, and Bryce wrapped his arms around her and rolled to protect her from the hard cement floor of the pool. He could hear her shriek under water and she gained her footing first, pulling him by the lapels, and pushing to the surface.

When they broke through they were gasping for air and she still had a hold of his jacket.

"You okay?" Ciara asked above everyone else's amused laughter.

"A little damp," he said calmly, feeling as if it had been weeks since he'd been this close to her.

"Good." She let go of his lapels with enough force to send him stumbling backward. "Serves you right for sneaking up on me."

"I didn't sneak. I was just standing there," he said to her back as she waded toward the stairs. His gaze fell on her round behind, then traveled upward. Not another woman on this planet could do justice to that low-cut one-piece, he thought. It gave him visions of what she looked like without it.

Ciara could feel his gaze on her, burning her and she tried to ignore it, looking at Carolina. The dark-haired baby was holding on to the rim of the playpen and bouncing up and down. Then Ciara saw Hope, Portia and Katey, each with a big smile. She sent them all a sour look and climbed out of the pool.

Bryce pulled off his shoes and tossed them on the cement deck, then followed Ciara.

"Hi sis," he said to Hope as he stood dripping on the pool tiles.

She grinned. "Nice entrance."

"You should have warned her I was there."

"How were we to know she'd turn on you like that?" Hope said, still smiling.

"Yeah, Bryce, just what did you do to make her so defensive?" Portia asked, glancing at Ciara.

"Nothing," she answered for him, throwing a towel at him.

Bryce dragged the terry cloth off his head and frowned, wondering what she was so hot about. He was the one who had just ruined an expensive suit and now looked like a fool in front of four women.

"Shouldn't you be at work? Hauling nets, selling mackerel," Ciara said, wrapping a towel around herself, then picking up the high chair. She opened it under the shade, then sent him a tight look before she headed back to the house for Carolina's lunch.

Hope scowled at her brother. "She's steamed at something."

"I don't think she likes surprises." Bryce sloshed to his daughter and lifted her in his arms. Carolina shivered at the cold contact of wet clothes, but Bryce was rewarded with a sloppy kiss and a hug. He settled her in the high chair, then strapped her in.

From inside the house, Ciara watched Bryce. His suit was ruined and she blamed herself. Then she blamed him for startling her. It was instinct to defend and too late she remembered she didn't have to around here. Resting her elbows on the kitchen counter, she cupped her face in her hands and let out a long breath. The man unnerved her. She wouldn't admit that aloud to a living soul, but he did. Just looking at him made her realize what she was missing in her life. The long hours of surveillance, the meals out of a bag and the bottles of antacid to cure the aftereffect. She lifted her head, watching him chat with his sister, hold her children and then talk with the other women. Something touched Ciara deeply when the women defended her, offering friendship to a stranger just because she was caring for Carolina.

His child.

Ciara's throat tightened, and the longing in her swelled. She forced it down, angry with herself for letting it surface. She remembered her job, her career, the years she'd spent climbing the corporate ladder to get where she was today in the CIA. Her job was a thrill ride of danger and intrigue, of solving crimes that effected millions. It was honorable. A duty to her country.

The familiar prickle of excitement coursed through her and she thought of returning to what she did best, of wearing a weapon and giving orders and catching the bad guys. It wasn't gone, she thought, that need, and she decided if she could just keep Bryce out of her mind, she'd be fine.

Then what, a voice asked, about your heart?

Boy, she thought, picking up the baby's lunch plate. She really needed to get back to her real job. Soon.

Bryce looked up as she walked outside and moved to his daughter.

"Here, be a dad." She handed him the plate of baby food.

He gave it back. "I have to change and get back to the office."

"Why did you even come by then?"

"I intended to join my daughter for lunch and didn't expect to go headfirst into the water."

"Your fault, Ashland, not mine."

"You're deadly with a high chair."

Ciara almost smiled. Almost. "Say goodbye to daddy, sweetie," Ciara said to Carolina, pulling a chair beneath her.

She started feeding the baby.

His sister frowned at him, yet her friends just smiled.

Bryce felt like an outsider.

Carolina squawked and held up some food for him. Bryce bent low and ate it off her fingers.

A chorus of disgusted "ews" followed, but Bryce didn't care. He smacked his lips for Carolina and she grinned, showing the white of two new teeth about to break the skin.

"Don't believe a word my sister says," he whispered to Ciara.

"What makes you think we talked about you?"

"I know her, I lived with her. She's naturally nosy."

"Any other instructions?"

Bryce felt the chill in her words. "Yeah, loosen up or I'll kiss you right now."

Ciara's eyes flared. "Don't threaten me, Bryce."

"It wasn't a threat." He eyed her.

Suddenly she smiled, but it was staged, too brittle, as if to prove to him that she'd do anything to keep what they shared suppressed.

It was like a sharp knife to his side.

He kissed his daughter goodbye, then straightened. Bryce tore his gaze away from Ciara's, then looked at his sister.

Portia and Katey made no bones about their curiosity, but Hope simply stared him down.

"Nice to see you ladies. Have fun."

"We will. More than you will, I guess."

"Don't track water into the house Bryce," Ciara called out. "The maid cleaned today."

"Yes, ma'am," he said and tossed her a smile that hit her like a strike of blinding light. Ciara returned it, her mental orders not to give an inch flying right out the window.

Hope grabbed Bryce's hand as he passed and he met her gaze. "What's going on between you two?" she asked.

"Nothing, like she said."

"Liar. You can cut the tension with a hacksaw."

"Butt out, little sister."

She arched a brow, like she did when they were kids and she imagined herself older and more learned than he was.

"Don't stir up trouble."

"Looks to me like it's already brewing. She's a nice woman, Bryce, and if you chose to come out of this self-imposed seclusion with her, be careful."

"Warning me off?"

"Of course not. But you've felt the need to carry the burden of Diana's death to the extreme, like you caused it."

"I did."

Hope shook her head sadly, moving farther away from the group. "Did you forget that I knew Diana? That she wanted to be introduced to you. Did you know that after your one and only date she talked about the two of you like your whole future was planned?"

His features yanked taut and his voice lowered. "Why didn't you tell me this before?"

She reared back. "Like you'd have listened? She wanted what I had, what Portia and Katey do. A nice home, and a family. I don't think she cared who provided that for her or which order it came in. Good grief Bryce, why do you think I didn't introduce her to you when I'd known her longer than you were even married?"

His brows knitted and he thought for a second. "I just thought you didn't want a friend of yours dating me."

"You didn't date, remember? She showed up and you went to bed."

He felt the color rise up from his neck. But the truth of it was that she was right. He hadn't been interested in anything but sleeping with Diana. Maybe that's why he'd felt so rotten later. Diana had been a friend of his sister's and that put some pressure on him.

"It doesn't matter, Hope. I married her. She was carrying my child."

"I know, I know." She walked with him toward the back door. "But you didn't cause her death. The problem was hers, her body, not yours."

He opened his mouth to speak, then snapped it shut. He knew that, he wasn't a complete idiot where his late wife was concerned, but he went to bed with Diana with the intention of saying goodbye in the morning and ending it there. It was heartless, but the truth. If he hadn't taken her to bed, she wouldn't have gotten pregnant and gestational diabetes and toxemia wouldn't have killed her. If she'd planned to trap him into marriage, she'd done a fine job and paid a higher price than he ever could. But all that didn't change a thing. Because in the end, when she was dying, she'd hated him, not so much for ruining her life, but for never loving her.

"You aren't going to listen, are you? I can tell by that look on your face," his sister said.

"Oh, I heard, and I know if Diana had lived, we would have been divorced about now."

Hope eyed him. "I hear a very unpleasant 'but' coming in that."

He offered her a small smile. "I don't want to fall into that kind of mess again."

"Boy, are you a downer on marriage and life in general."

He chuckled to himself.

"I'm almost glad you haven't been around. I'd hate to have Chris hear that."

"Ahh, darlin', nothing could destroy the incurable infatuation your husband has for you." Bryce leaned and pressed a kiss to Hope's forehead.

She gripped his arms and whispered fiercely, "We've missed you, Bryce. What will destroy this black cloud hanging over your heart?"

Before he pulled back, before he thought about it, he opened his eyes. His gaze collided with Ciara's across the pool yard.

Her, his heart screamed. Her.

After Bryce had left for work and the baby was down for her midmorning nap, Ciara had used the satellite phone and computer to contact her boss. She'd come very close to not calling him at all, not wanting to know if Mark Faraday was caught and behind bars. That fact told her she was getting too comfortable. She'd called immediately and was not all that pleased that Mark had been located and the CIA was setting up a sting operation to catch him passing information. Ciara volunteered to be the bait, but her boss felt that Mark was already wise to her involvement and would flee the instant he saw her.

Especially since she was the only one who knew the details of his betrayal.

More than I care to, she thought, sipping tea while sitting on the living room floor. She watched as Carolina ignored the scattered toys and was content to walk back and forth in front of the sofa, holding on to the seat cushions. Smiling at the little girl's efforts Ciara leaned back against a stuffed chair and enjoyed the late afternoon.

She was tired and admitted that it was a different kind of exhaustion. A happy one. She wasn't groping for the bed at night, or drinking gallons of coffee to stay awake during an operation, but just a "satisfied, put in a full day" tired. She attributed that to her new friends and the constant activity since she'd met them a few days ago. Keeping up with Hope, Portia and Katey was a full-time job. They each might have had a career before the children, but the change in lifestyle hadn't stopped them from getting the most out of each day now. Bryce had been right about his sister, she was nosey. Not rude, but pushy enough that it took a few times of changing the subject to make the three women understand Ciara wasn't giving any information. Besides, she thought, keeping secret that she had known Bryce before was more than just wanting privacy. It was preserving a moment in time.

Especially when she hadn't seen him much in the past couple days. Since the day he'd fallen into the pool, he'd been working long hours and stumbling in late, barely getting a chance to see his child. When he could stand being in a room with Ciara, he questioned her about his daughter, said good-night to his baby, and often skipped dinner to go to his room.

She didn't think he slept much, though. Often she heard him prowling the house and the temptation to go to him nearly overpowered her enough that she felt that strapping herself to her bed would be the only way she wouldn't. She shook her head, wondering if she was just being jittery. He made her feel so vulnerable that avoiding each other was just fine.

No, she thought, it's not. Not for Carolina.

She missed her daddy, cried for him and Ciara felt lousy that the conflict between her and Bryce kept him from his baby.

Her gaze slid to the windows, her brows drawing tight when she heard the sound of a car engine. Setting her cup on the coffee table she walked on her knees to Carolina, wiping the baby's chin and wondering when those teeth were going to cut through. Carolina ignored her ministration, shifting down the length of the couch, and when Ciara scooted back, the baby turned toward her. She was several feet away, her hand reaching out to her.

Ciara started to go to her, then stopped. Carolina held on to the sofa cushion with one hand.

She's going to walk, Ciara thought

The front door opened. "Ciara," Bryce called.

"In the living room," she said, trying to keep from startling Carolina.

He came into view and she whispered, "Get the video camera. I think she's going to take a step."

Instantly, Bryce set down his briefcase.

"It's in the hall closet by the stroller," Ciara said, and watched the uncertainty skate across the baby's face. "Hurry."

"I am. I am." Bryce went to the closet, retrieved

the camera and loaded it. He came down on his knees, focusing.

"Switch places with me," Ciara said.

"What?"

"Let me shoot." She reached for the camera. "You hold your arms out to Carolina."

He gave her the camera, then knelt down in front of his daughter. "Hey, princess," he said. "What are you doing?"

He was rewarded with a jumble of baby talk and a very distinct da-da.

"Oh Bryce, look at that smile."

Carolina let go of the sofa, cooing at her daddy, her arms out for balance as she trotted her first hurried steps toward him.

"That's it honey, come on." She took two more steps, then tumbled into his arms. Bryce grabbed her up and howled with laughter. "Did you see her? She's a pro already!"

Setting the camera on the coffee table, Ciara rushed close. "What a good girl!"

The adults kissed and hugged Carolina, and when Bryce laughed and held the baby up above him, telling her how proud he was of her, Carolina blinked at them, tears filling her eyes. Her lip curled down.

"Uh-oh," Bryce said, holding her close as Carolina burst into tears.

"Oh dear," Ciara said with a smile, her own eyes glossy. She stroked the baby's head, whispering soft words of praise. The baby sniffled and finally looked between the adults. Ciara clapped softly and the baby mimicked her. Ciara bubbled with laughter and she bent and kissed her charge.

When she straightened, she met Bryce's gaze, grinning. "Something, huh?"

"Yeah," he said his gaze sketching her features. She was so close he could smell her perfume.

"She's been practicing all afternoon. I was hoping she'd wait 'til you got here."

"Thanks for letting her come to me."

"Well, it's only fitting that I do the work around here and you get all the fun stuff," she teased.

"You're done a great job with her, Ciara. Thank you."

"You're welcome." Ciara's gaze searched his and when she started to move back, Bryce slipped his hand behind her neck and pulled her toward him.

She braced her hands on his chest. "Bryce, I don't think—"

"Don't think, Ciara. For God's sake, don't. I'm not."

His mouth pressed warmly to hers and she moaned at the warm contact, trying, in her mind, to resist, yet her heart refused to be ignored. She wanted this man. She wanted more than she had a right to, but that didn't stop her from sinking into his kiss, worrying his lips until he crushed hers beneath his own.

It was like coming home, a welcome back, soft and tender and filled with banked passion. *Oh, how I've missed him,* she thought and gripped his shoulder, longing for the feel of his strength against her, for the moment when she couldn't tell where she ended and he began.

His kiss grew stronger, his head shifting back and forth to take more and give more.

Bryce felt as if he were drinking in pure joy. She'd

driven him insane with desire for those first days and now he was just plain hungry for the sight of her. For the sounds she made, to be close enough to hear her breathing, feel her warmth. Carnal pleasures were outweighed with his want of her, of the woman, to uncover her secrets and share some of his own. He hadn't wanted to feel this way, hadn't wanted to get involved with her, but he admitted that she'd invaded him for five years and there was no use in battling for twenty more. He deepened his kiss, pushing his tongue between her lips and she answered with a deep throaty moan that set his nerves endings on fire.

It wasn't enough. He needed to feel her skin and reached...

Carolina squirmed between them, crying out her discomfort, and slowly they parted, stealing short quick kisses before looking down at the baby in his lap.

"Da-da! Moooo," the baby said, smiling.

Bryce blinked. "Is she calling me a cow?"

"Better you than me," Ciara muttered, her mouth and body tingling from his kiss.

He lifted his daughter off his lap and set her on the floor. Carolina immediately tried to stand and plopped down on her behind.

"I've got a few days before she starts running at least."

Bryce didn't say anything, his gaze shifting from his daughter to the woman he wanted more than just in his bed. He wasn't sure where this relationship was going, but he wasn't willing to discard it, either. Staying away from Ciara had given him nothing but sleepless nights and endless days of work trying to push her image out of his mind. But she was ingrained there. Lately, he found himself reasoning out why he should open this dangerous door more often than listening to the warnings of the past year.

Wanting her body beneath his had little to do with it. It was the woman she was, his mind finally separating a one-night fantasy from the real person kneeling on the floor with his daughter. He looked forward to glimpses of her, and conversation with her no matter how stilted. And for some reason, seeing her with his daughter made him want her more. Bryce still wasn't certain he wanted to take a chance and he would settle for simply being near her. Without fighting, without pushing, and hopefully she wouldn't close him out.

Because he didn't know what else to do.

Ciara had haunted him for five years, and ignoring the ghost of his past was a hell of a lot easier on his heart than ignoring the flesh-and-blood woman.

Especially when all it took was one look from her to grab him by the throat and hold him hostage.

"Bryce?"

He cocked his head, his gaze sliding over her. "Yeah."

"Watch Carolina. Dinner is ready." The timer sounded in the background. Ciara barely heard it. He was looking at her as if he wanted to swallow her whole.

He stood and offered her a hand up. She accepted and the motion brought her against him. He didn't wrap his arms around her like he wanted, didn't kiss her like he wanted and simply said, "You're dining with us, right?"

She hesitated for a moment and he felt his own breathing stagger.

"Sure," she said, a little lost when he smiled at her like that.

"Okay, I'll chase Carolina," he said, loosening his tie. "While you serve dinner up."

He went after his daughter as Ciara turned toward the kitchen, pausing once to frown back at him and wonder what was going on.

Neither of them were known for their restraint.

And when he was this close, Ciara felt like a thread about to snap.

Seven

Don't think. I'm not, he'd said.

Ciara *had* thought, she had kept her guard about her. That kiss had ended gently. A normal lovers' kiss.

Except they weren't lovers.

They weren't anything except adversaries.

All through dinner he'd watched her, staring at her in a way she couldn't understand. She liked understanding, being completely involved, and informed of what was going on around her. It's what made her a good agent.

But right now she felt as if she were losing a grip on that. On her ability to judge quickly and stick by it. On her ability to size up a situation in seconds and take action. But with Bryce, he was worse than listening to interference on the satellite waves. Nothing but static.

She'd been in control all her adult life. Had been promoted quickly, recognized by the agency enough times to know she was good at her job. But she was also cautious and efficient.

Not cautious enough to learn about Mark, a voice in her head prodded.

Yeah, well, Ciara thought. No excuse there. Call it a bad hormone day.

Was she just having another string of those? She just couldn't figure out what Bryce was up to lately. He wanted her. She wanted him. They were adults. It should be easy. Like it was five years ago. But he hadn't been a father then. He hadn't been a widower who'd secluded himself in a southern mansion deep in the low country because he still mourned the loss of his wife.

Ciara wasn't stupid. His sister Hope had said that Bryce and his wife had known each other one night. He'd gotten her pregnant and had done the right thing in his book, and married her. Ciara wasn't surprised he did. He was an honorable sort of guy, but that didn't mean he hadn't adored her. Hadn't loved her madly.

Love, Ciara scoffed, had gotten her into trouble with Mark Faraday because it had long-term leftover feelings to deal with. Love, in her job, made her soft. And sleeping with Bryce Ashland wasn't wise. It would ingrain her deeper in his life.

Then she realized he had a life.

She didn't.

She fought the thought, telling herself she did have one, it was just as isolated as his had been, according to his sister, for the past year. Except Ciara's isolation lasted longer. The other day by the pool, she'd been downright rude to him and was angered that he'd stirred so much in her, angered that she didn't have, could never have what his sister and Portia and Katey had. Futures, families, long-time friends.

Heck, the only person she'd been in contact with from her past since she was twenty-two was Katherine Davenport and that was to get this job and hide.

Bryce lifted his gaze from his daughter and looked at her from beneath a shock of black hair. Those blue eyes hit her like a hail of arrows, nailing her taut nerves to the wall behind her.

He had that much effect on her. That much power. She didn't want it.

Yet in the same breath she admitted she craved it. She wanted to submerge herself in him and not come up for air until she was satisfied. 'Til she had enough of him to last her another five years.

Immediately she stood and gathered a few dishes, bringing them to the kitchen counter. She couldn't bear to look at him and not somehow regret her choices.

Bryce paused in feeding Carolina to study Ciara.

She'd been quiet since they'd sat down to dinner. Oh, they'd talked, but it was about everyone else, his sister, and his family. Carolina. But he could feel the tension radiating from her. He knew he shouldn't have kissed her, but it felt so natural to do it at the time. He hadn't wanted to think. He still didn't. As he'd decided earlier, he'd just not antagonize her, like he seemed to always do. He didn't want her to close him out.

He wanted Ciara open for him.

His lips curved as his mind took flight on that thought and he tried to redirect it. "Dinner was great, Ciara."

She glanced at the platters. "Yeah, it was, huh? Thanks. Haven't lost my touch, I guess."

"I bet this is a stretch from embassy work."

"I'll say," she said with feeling. "This is harder." But she enjoyed it and felt fulfilled. Weird, since that was the last thing she expected to feel being a nanny.

Carolina fussed. Loudly. Bryce lifted her out of the high chair as Ciara reached for her.

"No, relax," he said. "I'll bathe her and put her down."

Nodding, her gaze followed him as he left. Over his shoulder, Carolina whimpered for Ciara. She waved and blew her a kiss, her heart fairly exploding with love for the little girl.

She wondered what she would do when she had to leave.

Just the thought of never seeing either Bryce or Carolina again left a heavy ache in Ciara's chest. But the time was drawing close. It wouldn't take the agency long to work up a sting and apprehend Faraday. Yet the one thing that made her nervous was that Mark Faraday wasn't stupid. And he was still loose, out there somewhere and no doubt looking for her. He had to notice she wasn't around, although they'd been assigned to different teams in the past weeks before she recognized his behavior for what it was.

Finishing the dishes, she flipped on the dishwasher before she went around checking the doors and setting the alarms. She wouldn't take any chances. Not with the baby, not with Bryce. Her hands were shaking as she returned to the sunroom, to her favorite spot in the huge house. Her mind ran with thoughts of Mark Faraday finding her. Of him harming Carolina or Bryce. She dropped onto the sofa, staring out the window. The backyard was lit with flood lamps that covered the shadows and illuminated the water. Bryce's cabin cruiser rocked gently at the end of the pier next to the small johnboat. She was almost tempted to ask him for a ride in it, to see the low country from the water.

Anything, she thought, to stall this time with him.

Bryce stepped into the sunroom, knowing he'd find Ciara there. Yet he didn't expect to find her looking so sad. "Want some wine?"

She whipped around like a frightened animal. "Bryce," she gasped. "I didn't hear you." She clutched the throw pillow with a death grip.

His brows rose and he frowned. "Obviously. I'm sorry." He held out a glass of red wine and she accepted it, draining half. Then with a long sigh, she slumped deeper into the sofa.

"I needed that. Thanks." Lord, her nerves were a pitiful thing, she thought, all tattered and tender.

"You're jumpy this evening."

She absently fluffed the pillow. "No, you startled me. I thought you'd be longer."

"The walking wonder went out fast." He pointed to the ceiling and Carolina's room above them.

Ciara smiled tenderly. He beamed with so much pride, Ciara felt herself relax. Then he sat down beside her.

She eyed him.

Her constant suspiciousness amused him, and Bryce wanted to get to the root of it. Of why she shut him out all the time, why she couldn't trust herself around him.

"Hope tells me you left the Secret Service for your wife."

If a door could slam shut on his desire, that was it. His body instantly clenched and his expression darkened. "Hope has a big mouth."

"She was more concerned for me I think."

His lips quirked in a quick smile. "Yeah, she knows there's something going on here."

Something, Ciara thought. Yeah, that was about it. Something powerful, something strong. Something she shouldn't touch. Something she wanted badly. "Well? Is it true?"

He hesitated, not wanting to have this conversation with her, not now. But he found no way around it. "Yes."

Her voice lowered, soft and sympathetic. "You must have loved her a great deal."

"I didn't love her at all."

Ciara's brows shot up and she propped her elbow on the back of the sofa, and regarded him.

Bryce shifted deeper into the cushions and sighed. "I married her because of Carolina."

"I know."

Only his gaze shifted to her. "Did my big mouth sister tell you Diana had it planned."

"No, she didn't. What makes you say that?"

He told her what his sister had finally revealed, about Diana planning their life out, and that Hope thought Diana wanted a family and didn't care how she got it.

"Sounds like a lonely woman who needed a family."

"She was orphaned, so I guess so, but the marriage was a mistake. She was possessive and afraid to be without me, so I left the service." He stopped, shaking his head. "I tried to love her. I wanted to love her. She was carrying my child, for pity's sake. But I couldn't, and she ended up hating me." He scraped his hand over his face, hearing the insults and rage in Diana because he couldn't love her and she'd finally understood it. "I didn't blame her."

"Why?"

"I ruined her life! I got her pregnant and she died." He started to leave the couch, but she put her hand over his.

Instantly his gaze shot to their hands, his fingers curling into hers. What if he messed up her life like he had Diana's? What if he pushed and Ciara ended up hating him?

When he tipped his head back, Ciara saw raw emotion shaping his features. She realized this is what had been hounding him, this was what she'd recognized the other day when she mentioned a guilty conscience. She understood, for in her career, she'd been faced with the same torment. Compassion swam through her and she'd suddenly recognized moments when this affected him, how tight he held to it, even when he was flirting with her.

"Bryce, listen to me." She gripped his hand tightly as if it would make him see clearer. "You're looking at the circumstances, and placing blame. Diana died of complications and she would have if she'd been pregnant by any man. Whether you loved her or not. Accident or planned, it doesn't matter now. You can't change the past. She's gone, and you have the best part of that marriage in Carolina.''

Bryce held her gaze with his own, sinking into it, into her, and a wave of comfort washed over him. He didn't know if it was her understanding or the simplicity that she saw, only that he heard her. Because he was ready to hear. ''Yeah, I do,'' he said quietly.

''And there is one thing I know for sure...''

''What's that?''

''I've been in your bed. I know she wanted to be there.''

His lips curved slowly, his smile devilish and growing by the second.

Instantly Ciara wished the words back, knowing she'd just opened up a subject she'd warned herself to keep closed. ''Forget I said that.'' Twisting away, she set the wineglass down.

''Can't,'' he said, his gaze traveling over her.

''Try harder, please.''

Before he could stop her, she left the couch, moving to the other side of the room. Bryce could feel her closing all doors and battening down the hatches against him. He wasn't going to allow it. Not again.

''And if I don't want to?'' he said.

''You don't have a choice.''

He gave her one of those sexy grins that liquefied her knees. She locked them and looked toward the doorway.

Bryce had the urge to make a dive for her just to keep her there.

"You don't have one, Bryce," she warned and sounded pathetically weak to her own ears. "Can't you just let a five-year-old affair go?"

His features tightened. "You think that's why I want to be with you? Because of Hong Kong?"

He was looking at her with such earnest shock her next words came out more like a question. "Why else?"

"Lady, have you got it wrong."

She folded her arms over her middle and cocked her hip. "So tell me how, then?" *Good grief,* her sensible CIA mind shouted. *Don't go there. Don't.*

"I'll admit that I haven't forgotten about that night. I can't and I don't want to. It was one of those once-in-a-lifetime moments."

"Yeah well. Once." She wouldn't admit aloud that she'd relived it over and over until, when she was alone, she could almost taste him on her mouth. His gaze moved over her, slowly, purposely and Ciara felt her insides jingle. "I'm no different—"

He shook his head slowly. "Before, you were just a figure, a face and a touch." He saluted her with the wineglass. "Now I know the woman."

He knows only part of me, Ciara thought, and the secrets she kept sent guilt sliding through her. "Okay, I'll give you that, but you must admit that night has colored your opinion of me."

"Yes, it did. Then."

She shouldn't ask. She wouldn't. She did. "And now?"

His gaze roamed her. "Let's just say it's changed."

"Unfair. That could mean a lot of things." And his

opinion meant a great deal to her. Right now, it meant everything.

"I'm not going to fill your head with compliments."

"Why not?"

He grinned and her stomach tightened. "Do you want to know that when I see you with Carolina I can feel your love for her?"

Her expression turned tender. "Of course I love her."

"Or that when you look at me, I can't breathe sometimes," he said as if she hadn't spoken.

Same here, she thought wildly. *Same here.*

"I've tried to push you out of my mind since you walked through my front door, and I don't want to any more." He rose slowly and started toward her.

Ciara stepped back.

"Why do I scare you?"

Pride straightened her spine as she wasn't about to admit he did anything to her, but it was a lie. And she was telling enough of those already. "Because if this were just sexual, I might be able to handle it." Her voice trembled and she swallowed.

"But it's not, is it?" He held his breath.

She shook her head, and he kept coming toward her, slowly, like a lazy prowl. Stalking.

Please don't touch me, she prayed. "You said you didn't want this," she whispered, taking another defensive step backward. "*I* said I didn't want this."

"Want and need are two different things," he said, his voice low and rough with desire. "And I need you, Ciara."

Her heart slammed against the wall of her chest

and she stared into his ice-blue eyes, thinking she wasn't what he needed, what he even thought she was. She wasn't forever after and carpools and kids. She wasn't dinner parties and family weekends. She was temporary.

And she was lonely.

God, she was so very lonely.

She was tired of it, and she knew what this moment meant. She could feel it tingling through her body and swelling through her heart. She'd been isolated for so long and being with him had changed that. There was freedom in his eyes as there had been that night in Hong Kong. Here, there were careless decisions and fun and relaxation, and she wondered exactly when she'd healed…and when she'd become so vulnerable.

She looked down at the floor, at their feet inches apart. The separating line in more than just their bodies. There was the final straw that would break them in half. If he knew she was a CIA agent, he'd hate her. The knowledge was instinctive. She'd lied—kept it from him and the danger that could touch his daughter. Deep inside she knew she was saving it for the moment when ties would have to be cut again and she would become Ciara Caldwell, not Ciara Stuart, and slip into her role of an operative for Central Intelligence. Oh God, she thought. Right now, it was the last thing she wanted to happen.

Which was it? her mind cried. Need or want. In those words he offered her the chance and the risk to her heart that she swore she wouldn't take again, with any man.

But Bryce Ashland wasn't just any man.

He was the only one she'd truly wanted.

With him, she could forget.

One step...one step.

"Ciara?" His fingers pushed under her chin and she lifted her gaze.

Her eyes were glossy with unshed tears, and at the sight of it, Bryce felt his chest cave, emotions folding in on each other. She looked helpless and fragile right now, so different from the strong and independent female who'd taken over his life, his thoughts. At that moment he understood just how hard she'd fought her feelings, fought her desire.

Then her lips trembled and Bryce experienced the rushing need to protect her, soothe her. "Darlin', talk to me," he whispered.

She took the step, wrapping her arms around his neck, her fingers sinking into his hair as she pulled his head down. "No talking, no thinking, Bryce." The words whispered against his lips and she shuddered. "Please."

Her mouth engulfed his, and she kissed him almost frantically as she pushed her body into his. It was like melting wax, need spilling from her and into him. It was as much a balm as it was torture and he closed his arms around her, and squeezed. She seemed to need it, to feel him more than ever before. It was as if they couldn't touch enough, feel enough and five years of fantasy flourished like a white water river out of control. He wanted to taste all of her. Not to match it with his past memory, but to erase the old and create fresh.

Suddenly she pulled back, breathing hard.

"What?" Then he heard it.

"Carolina."

Ciara was off like a shot, running through the house and up the stairs. Bryce was on her heels. She reached the baby first, gathering Carolina up against her and soothing her tears. His daughter shuddered and quieted, and Ciara rocked her in her arms, stroking her head and whispering gentle words. Bryce's gaze was riveted to her as he walked into the room.

She lifted her gaze from the baby to him and he saw her doubts. She'd had time to think. He was losing her so easily, so quickly, and panic filled him. He loved his daughter, but he needed this woman, more than in his bed. He had to have patience. But right now, he was out of it.

Carolina was already asleep in Ciara's arms and he took his daughter, laying her in the crib and covering her. Then he grabbed Ciara's hand, pulling her out of the room and closing the door. The sensation of urgency was tangible as he spun her into his arms and pinned her against the nearest wall.

Her hands flew to his chest. "Bryce?"

"No, Ciara. Don't. I know you. I know you're thinking of more reasons not to let this happen. But it's time to change things between us. Now."

Her gaze sketched his features, a million denials running through her head. But her heart spoke for her. "Yeah," she said, leaning closer.

He kissed her. Hard. A devouring kiss and thirsty for what only she could give. She responded wildly, unchecked, her hands gripping him fiercely, her body meshing to his. She gave as good as she got, and Bryce experienced the revelation of a lifetime.

No one would match him like Ciara. No one ever

had. Here, there was instant trust. Last time it was just sex. This time he'd make love to her.

And he'd show her there was a big difference between the two.

Eight

Ciara gave herself permission to want, to take, to have something she'd been denied. This man's loving. This man's touch. The way he made her feel so cherished and desired. Even when they were out of control

And they were getting there.

Fast.

And there was no turning back. Not without regret and she was full of those lately. She grabbed him by the shirtfront, pulling one side of the fabric tight and popping open each button, then yanking it from his trousers. All the while he kissed her, molding her mouth, his hands chasing over her body. She pushed the material off his shoulders and down his arms, then splayed her hands across his chest.

He flinched at the contact and met her gaze. She

could almost feel him tasting her with his eyes. A flood of fantasy and memory swept over her.

Impatient and greedy. Like she was now.

She forced him to walk backward, and kept pushing, intent on the bedroom she'd never seen. She hadn't wanted to see where he slept. Just the thought of it evoked too many images she couldn't fight.

Didn't want to fight.

"The bed that way?" Her chin nudged the air toward the bedroom.

"Yeah, if we make it that far." As they moved, he opened her blouse, sliding his hand around her to unclasp her bra. The instant he touched her skin, he lost it, pressing her to the doorjamb and filling his hand with her soft rounded flesh.

She moaned and covered his hands. "Are we there yet?" she asked over the loss of air in her lungs.

Bryce chuckled darkly and bent, taking her nipple deep into his mouth.

A deep throaty growl came from the back of her throat, and he knew she was watching him. It made his groin tighten unbearably to know it and when he licked and suckled her tender skin, he was rewarded with the most incredible sound. Breathy gasps, lush moans and his name chanted. He reveled in the sounds, let them coat him, feed his desire. With his tongue he drew tight circles around her nipple until her skin was damp and she was clawing at his shoulders. His hands were no less busy, opening her jeans, pushing them down, pausing in the task to dip between her thighs and heighten her pleasure. She was wet and hot, and the knowledge sent impatience rocketing through him. He stroked her and she frantically shoved at her jeans herself, working them down to give him better access.

Then he sank to his knees.

He buried his face in her taut stomach, his fingertips digging into her buttocks and felt himself tremble with want. He dragged his tongue over her smooth flesh and for a fraction of a second, glanced up. She was watching him again, her lungs working for every breath, her hands running voraciously over his arms, his face. Eager, hungry, lovingly. She smiled like a cat.

He peeled her open and tasted her.

She cried out, the throaty sound spilling over him, and he drove deeply, pulling her leg over his shoulder. She rocked and he felt her pulsing, her delicious squirming. It nearly undid him. Then he thrust two fingers inside her and she came apart for him instantly, her body tightening, pawing with the sweet explosion.

He devoured her pleasure.

Ciara couldn't catch her breath, he wouldn't let her. She jerked and flexed, her muscles tense and then she was falling, bathed in fast heat and throbbing pleasure. He moaned and flicked his tongue and she shrieked his name. He smiled, dragging his mouth across her thigh, biting her flesh, tasting her lush body all the way up to her mouth.

She was on him in an instant, kissing him, clinging to him. "Hurry," she whispered against his lips, shoving his trousers down. He made her this way she thought. Always so wild and hungry for him, for the slice of heaven only he'd given her.

"We need protection." He edged toward the nightstand beside the four poster bed, yet refused to give up kissing her.

"Don't need it." Her blouse and bra hit the floor.

He hesitated.

"Trust me," she said, pulling him back.

Bryce stripped out of his trousers, and Ciara took her fill of looking at him. His body was still rock hard, ropy with muscle and she stepped close until her breasts were touching his chest. He was breathing hard, staring down at her. "I'm about to throw you on your back and go to town." She smiled and smoothed her hands over his chest, then lower, feeling his muscles jump beneath her touch.

"No patience?"

"None."

She bent and licked his nipple and his breath hissed out between clenched teeth as she played over and over. He gripped her waist, wanting more and thinking he couldn't get any harder. Then she wrapped her fingers around his arousal and he thought he'd explode.

He muttered a curse and clasped her to him, kissing her thickly, cupping her buttocks and pushing his knee between her thighs. She ground down on him, her heat warming him, driving stinging currents of anticipation through his blood. He pressed his knee to the bed and held her there, suspended, hovering over her.

She stroked him, her fingertips sliding over the damp velvet tip of him.

"I want to taste you."

Every muscle he owned clenched. "No."

She smiled at the harshness of his voice and knew he was as volatile as she was.

Bryce thought he'd lose any ounce of restraint right there and pried her hand loose. Then she kissed him again, her lips, her tongue, her body rocking against his in sweet torture. Just the thought of being inside her, of feeling the velvet softness of her grip him was more than any man could handle. He ground his teeth and his shoulders tensed as he waited for a fraction of the rushing desire to recede.

He smoothed his hand up her side, enfolded her breast, then bent to draw her nipple into the heat of his mouth. He played and suckled, laved and tugged.

By the time he lifted his head, she was laboring for her next breath.

Cool blue eyes stared back at her. He hooked his hand behind her knee and spread her wider, his own thighs shifting between.

"Get ready for change, Ciara," he growled and she felt the challenge of his words prick her like needles.

He was laying more than his body before her, giving more than the physical. And Ciara knew that though she was temporary, her feelings for this man were not. She wanted more than she had a right to take, yet she answered him by cupping his face and kissing him thickly, licking the line of his lips before pushing her tongue inside.

Bryce moaned like a man in agony.

"Then change me," she whispered softly, closing her fingers over his arousal. He tensed in reaction, and she stroked the tip of him against her softness. He cursed softly and she felt his body tremble.

Bryce slammed his eyes shut and let her toy with him. "I wouldn't dream of denying you."

With a heave he pushed her to the center of the grand bed, then crawled closer. She sat up, pushing him back on his haunches, then climbed onto his lap. His arms closed around her, his arousal thick and tight between them, the impatience of passion stretching their nerves taut. Her gaze locked with his, she enfolded him, guided him. A near violent shudder wracked him and pulsed into her. His throat worked and he gripped her hips. She inched closer, and in nearly painful increments, he slowly filled her.

"Ciara, sweet mercy." Bryce swallowed, trying to catch his breath and failing. He had never felt so exposed, barren, and smoothing her hair back off her face, he saw the same vulnerability in her dark eyes.

They were still, his body buried in hers. One, wrapped tight and strong. And he knew no other moment would equal this.

He flexed inside her.

"Oh Bryce," she whispered, her voice fracturing.

"Yes, I know, I know," he whispered and touched his lips to hers, gently worrying her mouth and struggling not to blurt out what was swelling inside his chest. She was the only one for him, he thought. And in the morning, he would be certain that she knew it. The realization stunned him and he buried his face in the bend of her throat. "Darlin'," he rasped. "I need you."

"Me, too." She didn't want to examine the feelings rushing through her and reveled in their closeness, his hands molding the curve of her spine, then settling on her hips. His mouth traced an imaginary path down her throat, her chest and she leaned back, offering herself to him.

In the middle of a kiss, he gave her hips motion. They went slow, measured, and Ciara felt every inch of him leave her, then fill her again.

Ice-blue eyes flared and darkened with each stroke. Blood hummed in her veins and she wrapped her arms around his neck, her forehead pressed to his. He pumped, never leaving her completely. As if to do so would break the spell.

She wanted to capture and hold the magic, and when her body cried out, he soothed it. Her soul ached and he held it tenderly. She was alone, had chosen to be, but he'd surrounded her with more than she ever dreamed, tempting her to rejoin the living. She wanted forever, but could have only a fraction of time. Her eyes burned, her emotions tattered and needy, and she kissed him hungrily, thrusting harder, reaching for more than the sweet oblivion he could give her.

"I can feel you pulsing," he whispered, the friction nearly unbearable and he pulled her legs up around his hips and laid her on the bed. With his arms locked, his body braced, he plunged thickly and withdrew, the tender cadence of their loving releasing to the primal need to claim. Her, him, each other. Her body rose to greet him, welcome him, and he thrust, finding the perfect match he'd lost years before.

Here, she yielded to him. Here, nothing else mattered

And as their bodies clashed in carnal pleasure, their hearts spoke.

Need. Want. Love.

Slick skin met and clashed. Softness yielded and gave, undulating like waves on the wild sea. The flames of passion spread and burned. He pushed and pushed, long and deep, sending her body racing to catch the elusive pleasure.

Then they caught it.

"Ciara," he choked as an exquisite climax roared through his body, scraping up his spine and shattering through him. Throwing his head back, he drove into her and touched her soul.

She clung to him as he set off a luxurious rhapsody of sensation in her. She bowed like a pale ribbon, and he ground into her, time and motion suspended as opulent pleasure rippled down her body to claim him. To latch onto his soul and steal it out of his chest.

She whispered his name over and over, and he heard tears in her voice, saw them in her eyes when he looked at her. The sight made his heartbeat stagger and he eased down onto her. Immediately she gripped him tighter, burying her face in his chest.

Ciara felt as if every emotion she possessed was hanging by a thread, unveiled by his loving. Gone was the memory of Hong Kong and in its place grew the tenderness of a lifetime. Her throat seized and she knew she was on borrowed time. That this would end and likely destroy her. And him. But she could no more stop it than she could stop a wave, stop breathing. He was in her blood. She wanted all she could have, even it they were crumbs.

He rose up, and met her gaze.

"You okay?" he said, his voice rough.

"Incredible," she said, tracing his features, the line of his lips. He kissed her fingertips, her palm, knowing nothing could describe what he was feeling, what had just happened between them. And as he carefully rolled to his back, taking her with him, he didn't think words would do them justice. Bryce wanted only to stay there with her locked around him like a second skin, and forget the world that moved and lived beyond this moment.

Ciara lay sprawled across his chest like a sated lion as she waited for her world to tip back into focus. His hands moved over her spine in slow circles and together they let out a slow breath so full of contentment and peace, that deep inside, it scared them both.

A short while later Ciara stirred. Bryce's fingers were in her hair, toying with it where it lay spread over his chest. She snuggled deeper and didn't want to move a muscle.

"Am I too heavy?"

He scoffed. "Not likely."

He sifted his fingers through her hair and finally she lifted her head, and met his gaze. Her insides twisted and jumped at the look in his eyes, full of pure masculine contentment and she inched up, loving his groan and how he curled to meet her.

He kissed her softly, an erotic play of lips and tongue that stirred her body and warmed her heart. When he drew back and settled into the mound of pillows, she propped her forearms on his chest.

"Hi."

His lip quirked. "Hey yourself."

"You have nothing to say?"

"Fishing for compliments?"

Now it was her turn to scoff. He didn't smile, yet

continued to stare, his gaze moving over her features. "There is no going back now."

"Who said I wanted to?"

He gripped her under her arms and dragged her up his body. "Good, because we're just getting started."

"Started on what, Bryce? Making love with me again?"

"Ahh, so you know the difference."

Her eyes grew suddenly glossy and she pushed his hair off his forehead. "Yeah, I figured it out."

He rolled to his side, hovering over her. "I want more than this, Ciara."

"Shh," she said, and put a finger over his lips. He nipped it. "Let's just take it one day at a time."

Bryce let out a breath. He wasn't expecting a commitment and she was right. One night, one time in bed didn't make it so. But the fact that he wanted one from her still startled him. "Well, this day isn't over."

She smiled and wondered where her strength had gone. That same strength she'd had in Hong Kong that had enabled her to walk away from Bryce. Her throat burned and she knew that she would have to leave, that she'd destroy this sweet peace, a peace she'd never known, and go back to her real life.

She was living on borrowed time.

And she'd give up almost anything if it was hers to keep.

His arms dug beneath her, scooping her close. His mouth was on her breast, his tongue flicking her nipple before he sucked it deeply into his mouth.

"You taste so good," he said, turning his attention to the mate.

"It's the body wash," she said dryly and only his gaze shifted to her, tender humor in his eyes. He blew on her damp nipple and it tightened.

His hand swept down her spine to her thigh and he drew it over his hip. His hardness pressed against her and between her thighs grew hot and slick.

He reached between them.

Suddenly she shimmied lower.

"Ciara?"

And lower still.

"Oh no, woman."

She pushed his hands away and ducked under the sheet.

"What do you think you're doing?" But he knew, oh, how he knew.

"Undercover work, secret agent man." She disappeared beneath the dark sheet and Bryce growled and arched as her mouth closed over him. He felt every touch, every inch of her against him, every stroke of her tongue and his body shuddered violently, until he thought he'd split in half.

He slammed his eyes shut as she took him deeper and experienced the heady rush of passion coming at him from all sides. He couldn't stand it and he grabbed her, rolling her onto her stomach.

"Bryce."

He loved the disappointment in her voice.

"You little witch," he growled in her ear. "How much more did you think I could take?"

"More, much more," she said in a soft laugh, the sound cut off when he slid his hand under her belly and between her thighs.

She shuddered and gasped as a biting hot tingling

pelted her skin, simmered in her veins. Her body tightened, muscles flexing and clawing and he chuckled darkly, teasing her more.

He leaned over her, whispering how beautiful she was, that he adored this untamed side she hid from everyone but him. That he could feel her pulsing around him.

Her motions grew stronger and Bryce responded to her, pushing, pushing.

"Bryce, oh please, oh please."

"Take me with you," he growled and shoved. Their climax was wild, fierce, sensation splitting through them, only to drag them back together. He clutched her, riding the waves of primal passion, their bodies answering each other in savage pleasure.

She gasped for air, closing her hands over his and holding on as the sensations ebbed and receded.

"Ciara," he said drawing out her name.

"Hold me, hold me," she said and swallowed her tears, no longer wondering how he could affect her so deeply.

"I will, darlin', I will," he said, wrapping her in the cocoon of his arms.

Ciara sighed tiredly, swallowing her tears and not willing to admit what they meant. Her gaze moved over the elegant furnishings and opulent décor of the master suite. Above them lay a canopy draped in dark green brocade, the heavy curtains making the large bed an island in a creamy cloud of walls and carpet. Moonlight spilled into the suite from a bank of windows and French doors leading to the private balcony. She didn't want to move to view the rest of the room, too content to remain tucked in the curve of his body.

Yet all of it forced her to see that Bryce had centuries of roots, stability and a family name to uphold.

She had no ties, no bonds.

She'd cut them years ago and though she didn't regret anything she'd done for her job, hovering over her head was that carefully worded sentence that would cost her a child she loved and the man who held her heart. She snuggled deeper into his embrace, hoping she was wrong, hoping he would safeguard her heart, and protect a woman whose job was to protect the world.

Nine

A little kernel of panic filled Bryce when he stepped out of his bathroom and found no trace of Ciara in his bedroom—except for her clothes strewn with his across the floor. Tying his robe, he went to find her. His daughter's crib was empty and he went downstairs. At the foot of the steps, he instantly caught the sound of Ciara's voice and the scent of frying bacon. He came around the corner to the kitchen and stopped.

She was at the stove, cooking eggs, and wearing sneakers, a tight pair of navy blue bike shorts, and a gray stretch tank top. Not a curve was concealed. Lucky him.

She glanced at the time. "As soon as your daddy comes down we'll be off," Ciara said to Carolina.

"Off where?"

She spun around, the spatula raised as if she were going to use it as a weapon. "Sweet heaven don't creep up on me like that!"

"I didn't creep. Did I, princess?" he said to Carolina.

The baby cooed, her mouth full of scrambled eggs.

Ciara moved the pan off the burner. "Oh, you're her father, she'll side with you," she said defensively.

Chuckling, he walked over to the baby and bent to give her a quick kiss, then looked at Ciara. "You aren't going out like that, are you?"

Ciara looked down at her clothes. "What's wrong with this?"

"It's revealing as hell."

"Prude."

His lips curved in one of those heart-stopping smiles. "That's not what you said last night."

"That was last night," she said and he tensed, waiting for the doors to slam close. For her to go cool as ice and shut him out.

She didn't, his heart picking up pace as she walked over to him, and tugged open his robe before sliding her arms inside.

Bryce felt something give in him. Like the floor beneath his feet, and he closed his arms around her and kissed her.

And kissed her.

"Good morning, darlin'," he said against her mouth.

"Mmm," was all she could manage when she could feel him growing hard against her. Her insides shifted, burned as he familiarized himself with the curves of her body. But before she blocked out any more of her life and hid away in that bedroom with him, she drew back. He wasn't finished and kissed her twice more, quick and deep.

"God, I want you again."

"I can tell." She rubbed her hips against him and loved his pained look. "But I'm going for a jog and taking Carolina with me in the stroller."

"Didn't get enough exercise already?"

"I'm ready for another workout with you, though."

He grinned, and when she rode her hands down over his bare buttocks, Bryce thought the counter was a good spot to make love to her again.

Then Carolina squealed, swiping at her tray and sending bits of egg to the floor.

"I think she's ready to go," Ciara said, giving the child a no-no look. When she looked back at Bryce, he wore the oddest smile. Stepping out of his arms, she picked up a cloth and started cleaning up the mess. Belting his robe, Bryce watched her for a second, then stopped her.

"Go on, I'll take care of it."

Her brows rose.

"I was doing this before you arrived, you know."

"Yeah," she said softly. "I know." And you will again, she thought and looked away before he could see her feelings on her face. She'd been so lousy at hiding them lately.

"How about a boat ride when you come back?"

"No little shrimpies waiting to leap to their death into your fleet of nets?"

"I'm the president. I can take a day off."

"Stand in the Oval Office and say that."

He grinned. "His days off were a Secret Service nightmare."

"Yours won't be." She smiled at the prospect of fun in the sun with him. "I'll run fast." She gathered the baby out of the high chair and walked out, saying, "Don't forget fishing poles."

Fishing? Ciara? Bryce dropped into a chair and snatched up a piece of bacon, thinking that in the past month, his life went from lonely, angry and guilt-ridden, to downright perfect.

Now if he could just get Ciara to trust him enough to tell him exactly what she'd been hiding since she got here.

Ciara opened one eye and spied Carolina. She was in the playpen on the deck of the cabin cruiser, the boat's blue tarp shielding her from the sun. Her father was at the stern of the boat, aft as he so clearly pointed out, setting the poles. She, of course, was sunning on the bow. The heat beat down on her and she exhaled, her mind drifting into a place of peace and relaxation.

The boat rocked gently on the water, the sensation lulling her into a balmy dream without thoughts of leaving. Enjoy this, her mind cried out like a lonely child. She exhaled, barely hearing Bryce talk to his daughter. A gull shrieked overhead and the breeze cooled her skin. Heaven, she thought.

"You look good enough to eat," he whispered in her ear.

She smiled, refusing to open her eyes. "There's lunch in the cooler."

He chuckled. "Rats."

Her shoulders shook with silent laughter. "Is Carolina okay?" she asked. "Do you think it's too hot for her?"

"She's going to live here the rest of her life. She best get used to the heat and humidity."

Ciara opened her eyes and rolled on her side to look at Bryce. He was inches from her face. "Oh, for pity's sake, Bryce. She's a baby. A gator would get overheated in this weather."

He chuckled. "I gave her some cold water to drink. She's having the time of her life with all those toys and playing with the water bucket."

Ciara shifted to look past him to Carolina, watching her make a valiant effort to pour water from one container to another and squealing with pride when she did it. "Good girl!" Ciara said and the baby looked up and gave her a toothy grin, her nose wrinkling adorably. "Mud pies are next, sweetie," she said as if Carolina understood her.

Ciara waved, and blew the baby a kiss.

The baby kissed her dirty palm and waved back with every muscle she had.

Bryce glanced between the two females, not for the first time seeing the bond they shared. His heart overflowed with pleasure over it. "She loves you, you know."

"I got that feeling," Ciara said warmly, then brought her gaze to his. She smiled. "I marvel every time she discovers something new. It's like seeing the world all over again. She changes every day."

"I don't want her to grow up so fast."

"Yeah, then you'll be beating off the boys with a stick."

He groaned. "Boys. Thank God that's far away."

"Only about sixteen years."

"She can't date 'til she's twenty at least. Maybe thirty."

She laughed. "Hah, she's going to be a beauty. Just try and stop the boys from knocking on your door."

"When did you first date?" Lord, he knew next to nothing about her past.

Her features softened. "Sixteen, I think. My dad was like a hound after a squirrel when the boys came into the house. I recall him saying something like, 'I have a gun and shovel. No one would ever find you.'"

Bryce chuckled, sympathizing with the man. "So where is he now?"

He caught the flash of pain in her eyes and she hesitated before answering. "He's dead. He and my mother were killed several years ago in a jet crash."

"Oh, God, Ciara, I'm sorry."

"Thank you. The worst of it was it was their first vacation alone in years." Ciara rolled to her back and closed her eyes, realizing she'd told him more than she'd intended. Her parents' passing was years ago, leaving her with her brothers for guidance and mostly, leaving her in charge of her younger sister, Cassie for a while. Mostly, forcing her to leave the company for a while to fill her mother's shoes. The last image she had of her family flooded her mind and her eyes burned. *Oh, I miss them,* she thought and knew it was because she was here, with Bryce and his daughter. In a normal life that wasn't really hers at all. It was like she was living 'what might have been' had she not gone into the CIA.

"Darlin', you okay?" Bryce settled in the corridor leading to the bow, close to where she was lying against the windshield. He touched her cheek, and she turned her face into his palm, kissing it, then lifting her gaze to his. The agony in her eyes was enough to slay him where he stood. "Ahh baby, I'm sorry." He gathered her in his arms. "I didn't mean to bring up old pain."

"It's okay," she whispered, clinging to him, loving that she had someone to share it with, someone who understood. She swallowed repeatedly, trying to keep back the grief she'd never had the chance to shed, for her parents, for the family she'd abandoned for the sake of her career. It was for their own safety, she told herself again. Their safety. Yet her heart wasn't listening and the dam broke.

A decade of tears shattered the stillness.

Bryce groaned and shifted to the bow, pulling her deeper into his embrace. Her shoulders shook as old heartache spilled in tortured sobs that cut him in half. He never really imagined her crying like this. She was so independent and strong, almost invincible. It was a long time before her sobs quieted. A lot of hidden sorrow, he thought and wondered if this was why she shut her emotions off so frequently.

When she was silent and still, he squeezed her, then nudged her head back, staring into her soulful eyes. Then he covered her mouth with his.

Their kiss was slow and tender, her heartache soothed under the balm of his attention.

"Thank you," she muttered after a long moment.

"I hate to see you hurting."

She sniffled. "I'm okay now." With the end of her towel, she blotted her eyes.

Bryce tipped her chin up, and could almost see her turning the pain away, marshaling her emotions and stuffing them into a compartment he knew he couldn't open. "Talk to me, darlin'."

"Nothing to say about it."

He drew on his patience and said, "You can trust me with anything, Ciara. Even your pain. You know that, don't you?"

She nodded and kissed him again, knowing she couldn't. Not with her secret. And right now, she needed him more than she needed to tell him. Not breaking the kiss she shifted closer, and let him work his magic. Their skin meshed, sun-scented and warm.

His hand rode down her back and enfolded her buttock.

Suddenly a horn sounded. They broke apart and looked to see a passing boat filled with people. They hooted and waved and someone shouted.

Ciara buried her face in his chest. "Good grief, I feel like a teenager caught necking by the school principal."

Just then Carolina cried. "Oh dear, the noise startled her," Ciara said and Bryce found his arms empty as she shifted off the bow and went to the baby.

She scooped Carolina up, soothing her tears and reaching for the little life vest the baby had to wear when she was out of the playpen. When Carolina felt sufficiently loved, Ciara slipped on the vest and sat down on the padded bench, reaching for the cooler. She pulled out a snack for Carolina and offered it to her. His daughter stuffed the crustless sandwich in her mouth in a very unladylike fashion.

Smiling, he folded his arms over his chest and studied the woman who turned his world inside out. She was resilient. He'd give her that. She was nothing like Diana or any other woman he'd met before. Last night in his bed, she'd felt what he did. He was sure of it. It was more than just changing things. More than needing each other and wanting that intimate connection. It was a mating of souls, he thought. As if he'd been searching for her, yet not knowing he *was* searching, and when he found her, it was a pleasure enough to kill him.

It was a little unnerving. And he wondered if he was up to this. To be strong enough for her, to be her match.

"Hey, want a soda?"

He focused on her. "A beer."

"Hell no, you're driving this thing," she said and tossed him a soda.

He caught it. "You could."

"I know I could, but I get hot seeing you standing at the wheel like a sea captain."

He grinned. "Let's get underway then." He popped the soda top.

She laughed and gave him a seductive smile. "Foreplay is everything, Bryce. Have some lunch with us girls and then take the long way home."

Home, he thought. She'd made his house that way. Before he and Carolina had been just living there, secluded. Now there was something better. Much better.

He sat down beside her, sharing sandwiches and

munching on chips, the baby between them and making more mess than any child had a right to make. Neither of them cared. They talked for what felt like hours, about Carolina, his business, the low country he loved so much.

"So," Ciara said, finishing off her sandwich and dusting her fingertips. "I never did ask, what's the name of your boat?" It was already in high tide water when she got in.

He hesitated and Ciara wondered if that was a blush she saw, or just too much sun. "The ships for the company are called the *Lady Carolina* and the—"

"Stop stalling, Ashland. I mean this one." And he knew it.

He didn't answer, smirking to himself. Frowning suspiciously, she set down her soda and went aft, sitting on the edge and hanging on to the ladder to lean down and look at the back.

She popped up, blinking. Stunned.

His smile was slow and almost lecherous.

"*Hong Kong Knight.* You named your boat after a night of sex!"

"After my most memorable one, yes."

"Oh, bet that kind of boasting went over real well with Diana."

Instantly she wished the words back. Yet his expression didn't change, telling her that he'd let that part of his life go.

"She never knew. No one did. Ever. It was my secret."

Ciara felt warmth explode inside her.

"And you?"

"Nope, though I do have one friend who suspects

and mentions Hong Kong just to see the look on my face.''

''What look was that?''

She stood and walked toward him, seduction in every cell of her body. ''Pure satisfaction.'' She stopped close and bent, giving him a delicious view of her bosom before she kissed him.

Her kiss had passion written all over it, in the way she outlined his mouth with slow deliberation, in the way she pushed her tongue between his lips, mimicking the dance they had done all last night.

His groin tightened and Bryce shifted in the seat, one hand steadying Carolina. He wanted to touch Ciara so bad, fondle all that flesh hanging out of her swimsuit. But there were just too many boaters around.

''Is it time to go home yet?'' he said when she eased back. She was breathing as hard as he was.

''Weigh anchor, captain. And take a shortcut.''

A few hours later, on the balcony under the stars, Bryce pushed into her, her body calling him back. A slick slide of passion and hunger that never seemed to weaken, only grow stronger, washed over her.

''Bryce,'' she gasped and lifted her hips to meet his strong thrusts, digging her feet into the floor.

His features were tight with desire, his body taut against hers as he thrust. Ciara pulled him down onto her, wanting to feel his pleasure and make it her own. He plunged and she smiled into his eyes as her body burst with satisfaction. Pure and loving. She arched, sweet rapture spilling through her blood, making it sing.

With one hand, Bryce held her off the floor and against him, gazing into her eyes as passion erupted, splitting through him and into her. He kept pushing, his gaze sweeping her body in the throes of her climax.

It was enough to make his eyes burn. To know he gave her pleasure, to know he'd found more than he bargained for when she walked into his life.

Several moments passed, their breathing and the wind the only sound filling the room. He lowered her to the floor and sank down onto her.

She moaned with contentment and he eased from her, rolling to his back and pulling her close. She wrapped her limbs around him, sighing.

Ciara stared up at the stars coloring the Carolina night, and her breath caught as one shot across the dark sky. "Make a wish," she whispered, pointing.

"I don't need wishes. I'm a very contented man."

She nudged Bryce. "And arrogant, too."

He shifted to look at her, tipping her face to the moonlight. "What did you wish for?"

"I'm not telling."

"More secrets?"

"What's that supposed to mean?"

"You hide things from me, Ciara. I don't care what they are, except that you don't trust me enough to tell me."

"There is nothing to tell, Bryce." Nothing that would make a difference, Nothing that would keep her from breaking her heart and his.

He kissed her forehead, not responding, then he settled her back in his arms as if they hadn't spoken.

Ciara's throat clamped tight and she hugged him, wishing again, yet knowing it would never come true. Nothing could make time stand still.

Ciara felt strange. It's not that she hadn't been in a grocery store before. But she never had with a baby strapped into the cart. Or a handsome man beside her. And she would have sworn a month ago that she would never have experienced a day like it in her life.

Bryce reached for a package of cereal and tossed it into the cart.

"You can't just toss it in, Bryce, or everything won't fit." She leaned over Carolina to resituate the package.

"Why don't I push and you shop? Or are you territorial about who has command of the shopping cart?"

Ciara made a face and switched places with him, handing him the list.

Bryce had to rush to keep up with her. She was moving down the aisle, going after exactly what she needed. "Have you been in this store before?"

"No why?"

"It's just...well...how the heck do you know where everything is? It takes me at least an hour."

"It's a woman thing," she said but knew it wasn't. Her CIA training taught her to take in several details in one sweep, the arrangement of obstructions, the nearest escape route, assessing the offense. At least she wasn't slipping, she thought, then glanced at the other women in the store. Some looked hurried, dealing with children's boredom. Across the produce aisle a couple strolled, a four-year-old talking incessantly. The sight of them hadn't bothered her until now.

Their lives, or what she'd imagined them to be, seemed so mundane and lifeless to her months ago. But now, she was just plain jealous, and resentment rose in her. What good was her career, she thought, if she wasn't truly happy?

And when did she stop being happy?

She lifted her gaze to Bryce.

When I fell in love with him, she thought.

Ciara looked away, not denying it to herself. She loved him. Oh lord, she hadn't expected to but she did. She didn't examine when it happened, it just did. And the thought of being without him was eating at her. It was as if she were waiting for her heart to be torn out. She hadn't checked in with her boss because she didn't want to know if the sting was over. Didn't want to go back to work.

She looked back at Bryce, walking closer. With him she knew what real happiness was, and she was just getting used to the taste.

The baby fussed and Ciara focused. "Oh, I recognize that sound." Immediately she went for a box of animal crackers, opening them and giving them to the baby.

"The whole box?"

"I say bribery is allowed when you're in a store. We're done by the way."

He sighed with what could only be relief and Ciara laced her arms with his. "Poor man, do you deserve a reward for behaving better than Carolina?"

He looked at her, half-offended, half-intrigued.

"Nah, you whined too much."

He chuckled. She walked ahead, placing the groceries on the conveyer belt.

A few minutes later they were outside. Carolina was still stuffing as many cookies as she could into her mouth. Ciara reached for the box, knowing she'd get a fight.

A shot rank out and instinctively Ciara threw herself over the baby and pushed the cart between two cars. She and Bryce collided as he did the same thing.

When they looked around and realized it was a car backfiring, Ciara let out a breath and checked the baby. Carolina just kept eating cookies.

Bryce stood beside the car, scowling at her.

"What?" She unlocked the trunk.

"Okay, that was clearly a defensive move, Ciara. I was trained by the Secret Service to do it." He folded his arms over his chest. "Just where did you learn that?"

Ten

Ciara stared, her expression blank. "It was a maternal instinct, I guess," she said, shrugging.

"Most people would just look to see what it was first, not cover a person and be ready to take a bullet."

"I'm not most people. I was with the Embassy, remember? And a bullet? It was a backfire."

She started putting the bags into the trunk. He didn't move, still staring at her. Not now, she thought. She couldn't tell him now.

"But neither of us knew that."

"True. Your instinct was to protect, just as mine was. It was a split second decision, Bryce, and though this is a small town, it's not immune to a holdup now and then."

His features softened a little.

She stopped putting the groceries in the trunk and looked directly at him. "What would you have me do? Stick my head up to look? Ignore the sound and chance Carolina getting caught by a stray bullet, or maybe getting hit by something as simple as a street-light snapping from its brackets?"

"Of course not."

"Then drop it. You're making a mountain out of a molehill. I would take any harm for this child," she said, stroking her hand over the baby's head. Carolina looked up at her, unaware of the tension between the adults, and smiling as she offered her a mushy cookie. "Isn't that enough?"

She lifted her gaze to his. And waited.

"Yes. It is."

She nodded and lifted the baby out of the cart, silently telling him to finish loading.

Bryce deposited the last bag in the trunk and shut the hood, watching through the window as Ciara strapped his daughter into her car seat, kissed her, then shut the door. Across the hood they stared at each other, and though what she said sounded logical, natural, he had his doubts. She'd been ready to pull that cart down on top of her for protection. She'd instantly moved between the vehicles for an extra shield.

Maternal or not, most people didn't know to do that. And most people wouldn't be thinking that fast on their feet.

"Want me to put the cart in the rack?"

He blinked and shook his head, pushing the cart into the rack and coming back to the car. She was already inside, twisting in the seat to talk to the baby.

And ignoring him.

He felt it and wondered why the incident had damaged something between them. She didn't like being questioned but then, he knew that from the start. As he started the car and pulled out of the parking lot, Bryce realized he needed some answers. And for the ride home he debated on pressuring her for them, or finding the answers out on his own.

For the remainder of the day Ciara went on as if nothing happened. As if she hadn't had a moment of complete and utter panic in the store parking lot. As if Bryce wasn't looking at her strangely. She fed the baby and took her outside to play, and though Bryce joined her, the conversation was a little stilted. She could feel his eyes on her, and not in a seductive way. He was trying to read deeper and it scared her.

She wanted so badly to reveal everything to him, to get it out in the open and go from there. She trusted everything about him, except his reaction. She couldn't, because as much as she loved him, she couldn't bear to see it destroyed. She didn't think she could take a rejection from him. And telling him could endanger his life.

Until Mark Faraday was caught she had to stay hidden and that meant hidden enough so that nothing would touch her or him and Carolina. She knew she should contact her boss, but each time was a risk and she really didn't want to put all her faith in her superiors. She was out of the loop, away from the workings of her team, and being uninformed made her vulnerable. But climbing back into the ring could make her a target, too.

She let out a long sigh and kept her gaze on the

baby, who was walking all over the place and shrieking with happiness about it. She glanced at Bryce. He was staring at his feet and she wondered what was going on in his head right now, then decided she would never know until he spoke up. She took a risk and pried open the can of frustration she could see building in him.

"What's eating you?"

"Nothing."

She rolled her eyes. "Come on, talk."

"You going to answer?"

"Sure."

He tipped his head back and met her gaze. "Where were you born?"

Well, that was out of left field, she thought. "Georgia."

"You don't have an accent."

"Lost it when people kept making southern jokes about me. I never did have the power that usually comes with it. You know the steel magnolia quality."

His lips quirked. "Any brothers or sisters?"

Ciara stared into those beautiful blue eyes and knew he wasn't testing her. He just wanted to connect to her. She tried to see herself from his point of view and the picture wasn't all that attractive. She saw a woman who was living on the surface of life. His life. Keeping him at arm's length. And she'd bet that was exactly how he was feeling right now.

She hesitated for another moment, considering the harm, and what he might do with the information. Because of her job, her family had different names than she did. Bryce knew her as Stuart, not Caldwell. She didn't think he'd run to his computer and start doing a search if he wasn't satisfied. But it came down to two questions. Did she love him enough to reveal some of her past to bring them closer? Or did she want to reveal it for herself?

Trust. With her heart, with her life? Ciara knew she'd never know until she took a chance. The price was great, yet her love for him was greater.

"I have two brothers, Michael and Richard, and a little sister, Cassie. She just graduated from college and is off traveling the world with fashion designers." At least she thought she was. "Mike and Rick own a construction company. They have families."

"So you lied to me?"

She reared back. "Excuse me?"

"You said your past was not important and too painful to talk about. Hell, I thought you were abused or something the way you hid it."

"It's past. What difference does it make now what school I attended, how many boys I dated?"

He set his iced tea aside and braced his elbows on his knees, the motion bringing him closer to her. "It's part of who you are, Ciara, and I realized I barely know you."

"You know me, you know who I am. God, how can you not!"

Bryce felt the hurt and defensiveness in her words. "Yes, I do know you. I know the woman who loves my daughter like she was her own. I know the woman who gets teary-eyed over dinner roll commercials." She flashed him an embarrassed smile. "The one who drives me wild with her touch. I know the woman who makes love with me like there is no tomorrow, when there is a tomorrow. If you'll just see it."

Ciara swallowed repeatedly, her heart thundering in her chest.

"But I don't understand what made you this way. I don't know how it is that you can turn your emotions off when you want to. And turn them on so brightly it makes my heart skip."

Her eyes burned. No one could read her like he could. No one before wanted to. She'd had to be more than businesslike in her career. As cold as men, as calculating as the snipers she'd been ordered to shoot to kill. Her stomach rolled at the thought and she realized that insensitive temperament wasn't so easy to dredge up and thrust out like a shield anymore. Staring into his eyes, she felt her heart weaken. To his pleas and to her need to share her greatest shame.

She swallowed a breath. "I did something that hurt them all, Bryce. And I thought it best to just stay away."

His expression first hardened, then softened. "What happened?"

I joined the CIA, she thought. She went off and dismissed them from her mind, from her heart. "I abandoned them."

"Why?"

She licked her lips and spoke the truth. "Because when my parents died I got all the burdens my mother had. I was mother to Cassie and being a housewife to two men, yet with no husband. They had their lives and were going full steam ahead, yet expected me to stay home and hold down the fort, make it as if my parents hadn't been blown to bits in a crash!" She choked on her breath, and stood suddenly, folding her arms over her middle and walking a few feet away.

She watched Carolina walk unsteadily and try to gather up her pail and shovel. "I was young and wanted freedom, too. I wanted them to pay attention and see that I was drowning. That I was losing the chance to have my own life and living my mother's instead."

Her throat closed and she bit back scalding tears. She'd been so angry with them for so long. Angry enough to push them out of her heart and focus on the career that made a difference in the world. Yet when she'd arrived here, when she'd fallen in love with a needy baby and a lonely man, she let herself feel.

And now she was feeling so much she couldn't breathe.

Bryce watched her shoulders tighten and knew she was fighting her emotions. "Don't blame yourself. They had a part in it."

"I'm the one who left."

"But whether they knew it or not, they pushed you out." He stood and came to her, tipping her head back and staring into her sad eyes. Sympathy swam through him. "I understand."

"Oh yeah, right."

He smiled slightly, patiently. "I do. I'd been expected to take over the family business, but I didn't want to. And my father knew it. He just kept ignoring my wishes. When I went into the Secret Service, my father was more than disappointed. He'd accepted it, expecting me to return home someday and be a part of the company. But if it hadn't been for Diana I would never be the president right now."

"But you didn't cut them out completely."

"Yes I did. I never came back. Not until my father became ill and was considering retiring. That's really why I was home when I met Diana. Otherwise I'd have never come home."

"I doubt that."

"Thanks for the confidence, darlin', but I'm sure my sister blabbed that I hadn't exactly been the social butterfly when I came back anyway."

Her lips curved gently. "Yes, she did blab that much."

"I resented the hell out of my family even mentioning I should come home permanently. Maybe I even held it against Diana for forcing me to."

"That's a whole other issue, Bryce."

"And a dead one." He pulled her closer, wrapping his arms around her, and hers clamped his waist. He held her, feeling her sorrow shudder through her, and she sighed, snuggling into his body. He rubbed her back in slow circles.

"It okay, baby. I'm sorry I pushed."

"No." She squeezed him. "You deserved to know." And she wanted him to.

She tipped her head back and accepted his kiss, the heady warmth of it spreading through her like sweet wine.

Carolina trotted up and grasped their legs, trying to hold on and not totter backward. Ciara bent down and scooped her up. Carolina offered them a rock.

Ciara thanked her and held it to her chest like it was a diamond.

Bryce watched their interaction, wondering how he could see the truth of her love so plainly, yet still have this niggling suspicion there was more to her

than she'd revealed today. He resented the thought
and in an effort to push it out, he kissed her, feeling
a bond that went deeper than his soul when his daughter clutched at them both.

In the garage, Bryce climbed out of his car, turned
off the house alarms, then stepped inside. Immediately he switched the alarm system back on. He'd
tried to get home earlier, but it just wasn't happening
today. At least he managed to get home before sunset
the past three nights, he thought, then frowned at his
house. It was dark, with only a small lamp lit in the
foyer. He called out and when no one responded, he
checked his watch. Where could they be at this hour?
He moved through the house, through the kitchen,
sunroom and out onto the pool deck. It was empty
and he spun around and searched the first floor, room
by room, then took the stairs two at a time.

He thrust open the door to his daughter's room. Her
crib was empty, the lights off. A vise clamped down
on his heart, and he rushed to Ciara's room, finding
it too, empty and dark. He yelled for her.

And he didn't get a response.

Bryce rushed from door to door, shoving them
open and finding his house horrifyingly barren of life.
He returned to Ciara's room and opened her closet, a
little spark of hope coming when he saw her suitcases.
Over his harsh breathing he heard soft music and he
nearly tripped over his feet as he turned toward her
private bathroom door.

With panic still riding him like a hurricane, he
thrust open the door and froze.

Ciara flinched, holding his daughter to her chest.

She was in the tub, a sea of bubbles surrounding both females.

He let out a long relieved breath. "Thank God." He rushed forward, sinking to his knees as he cupped the back of Ciara's head and brought her to him. His mouth crushed over hers, his kiss hard and utterly possessive. She responded hungrily, soothing his terror with the heat of her mouth.

"What's wrong?" she said when he drew back.

Words spilled from him in a rush. "When I came home the house was dark, I couldn't find you and thought that—" He touched her face, his daughter's head as she splashed water. "Hell I don't know what I thought."

His hands were trembling, Ciara realized. "You thought I left with her?"

His gaze shot to hers. "No. Not a chance. I thought something happened to you. Both of you."

A spark of warmth spread through Ciara and just as she recognized it, she realized how she'd feel if anything happened to them. "We're fine. Oh, close the door, Bryce, the draft is making Carolina shiver."

He did, sagging to the floor and letting the horrible images of the past moments fade. Then he started to notice...things. Ciara's long hair piled on top of her head. The sheen of her wet skin, the swell of her breasts as his daughter snuggled against her, the bubbles on her chin, on his baby, and the way they looked together, as if they belonged. A hard brittle ache settled in his chest.

"What the heck are you doing in the tub together anyway?"

"Relaxing. Pampering ourselves." She looked lovingly at Carolina. "We *are* girls, you know." She cupped warm water and poured it gently over Carolina's back and head.

His daughter patted the water. "She cries when I give her a bath."

"Do you get in with her?"

"No." He looked at her as if it was the furthest thing from his mind. Which, at the moment, it was.

"I guess," she said, shrugging, "it's the lack of security she feels in the tub. She cried the first couple times with me, too. But she's been in the pool and is used to the water now. See." Ciara poured water over the baby's head. Carolina squinted and blew it out of her mouth, but didn't cry.

Bryce smiled, inching closer. "Hey, princess."

As if just noticing him, Carolina launched toward him, her arms outstretched. Bryce lifted her out of the bath water, settling her on his lap.

"You're going to ruin another suit," Ciara said softly.

"Who cares." He wrapped the baby in a towel and spoke to her, asking about her day and when she just made noise, he agreed and smiled. Ciara's heart swelled and tightened in her chest. Her eyes watered a bit and she understood how hard Bryce was trying to be mother and father to his little girl and how much he loved his daughter. She'd known that he did, but seeing it pour from him was another matter entirely. It made her see how much she wanted to stay right here and be a part of it.

He kissed his baby, settling her on his lap. "She done being pampered?" He inclined his head to Carolina.

"Actually no. We have to rinse the bubbles off or her skin will get dry." Ciara opened her arms for the baby and he put his naked child in her arms.

Their hands folded over each other to get a better grip on the slippery infant and Ciara lifted her gaze to his.

He looked at her differently somehow. She couldn't quite put her finger on why it was different, it just was.

"Look how she trusts you." Carolina laid her head on Ciara's chest and jammed her thumb in her mouth. Ciara continued to drizzle water over the baby. "Next time use the tub in my bedroom. It's bigger. And the whirlpool makes great bubbles," Bryce said.

"Sure, but I'd rather just have you in the tub with me." Ciara wiggled her brows. "Could be interesting."

He groaned with frustration and though he was reluctant to leave, he climbed to his feet. He stared down at her, at his baby against her breast, at the blanket of bubbles cloaking them.

"Call me when you're done," he said reaching for the doorknob. "I want to put her to bed."

"I'll be just a few minutes, she's already sleepy."

Bryce looked back, his body growing harder at the sight of Ciara. "I'll be close." She nodded and he stepped out, pulling the door closed.

Ciara looked at Carolina, then slid deeper into the water, warming the child and admitting that the moments just past felt incredibly normal and what they did for her tired soul. In the past couple of days since she'd told Bryce about her family, they'd fallen into a routine. Like a family. She did all those things she used to hate, but because they were for Bryce and Carolina, she didn't mind. Though she was really glad he could afford a housekeeper. It gave her more time for them.

Thoughts of returning to her real life grew more distant and though she knew her boss was wondering what had happened to her, she didn't care. She could keep that locked out forever, but the fact that she was keeping it from Bryce gave her doubts as to how long this would last. Especially when she was falling more in love with him every day.

Downstairs, Bryce was halfway through the meal Ciara had left for him when he realized she hadn't come down. Leaving the table he went upstairs and when he pushed open the door to Ciara's room, he smiled tenderly. Ciara and Carolina were snuggled together on the bed, the baby tucked under Ciara's chin. His daughter's little fingers were wrapped around a lock of Ciara's hair as if she was afraid she'd leave her. Bryce understood, because he was having those feelings himself. Not knowing what to do about it right now, he stepped close, untangling his daughter and lifting her into his arms. He went to her room, putting her in her crib. She fussed for a minute at the loss of warmth, then settled.

Bryce went back for Ciara.

Scooping her in his arms he carried her to his bedroom. Instantly she woke.

"Bryce?" she said on a yawn as he laid her on the bed.

"Shh." He lowered the lights and stripped out of

his clothes. "I want to sleep with you, darlin'. Just sleep."

She slipped out of the robe and reached for him, pulling him down on top of her. "You sure it's just sleep you want?" she said, moving against him.

"Yes." Was that gallant, or what, he thought?

Her hand snaked under the covers. "Can't I interest you in more?"

He rolled on top of her, his arousal pushing against her softness. "I'll always want more from you... always."

Eleven

"**H**oney, would you grab the potato salad?" Ciara called as she headed out the back door.

Bryce grinned and did as she ordered, following her onto the pool deck.

"Honey?" Hope said when he was outside, her baby on her hip.

He looked at his sister, deadpan. "You want me to say you were right, don't you?"

"Oh, yes."

"Okay, you were."

Hope smiled at the sky. "Ahh, sweet justice."

"Now keep your mouth shut."

"I swear." She crossed her heart to prove it.

"Oh, yeah right, like I believe that."

"Believe what?" Ciara said coming back for the bowl of salad.

"That Hope could keep her mouth shut."

"Not a chance. That's what makes her so interesting."

Hope stuck her tongue out at her brother.

"I'm going to stand at the hot grill and repent," Bryce said dryly.

"Yes, man kill food, man burn food," Hope said.

"Yeah and women clean it up," Ciara added.

He winked at her, running his hand over her waist as he passed.

Bryce laid out the hamburgers and hot dogs for the kids, the steaks for the adults, then shut the grill. His gaze scanned the pool yard.

Children played in the shallow end, their parents scattered about the deck, keeping a sharp eye on them. The air was peppered with "mommy watch, daddy look at me," and Bryce couldn't wait for Carolina to be chattering away like that. Almost. His daughter, who was the most fascinated of the group, was in the shallow end of the pool, her body surrounded by a seated rubber ring float and looking like a stuffed pumpkin with that orange life vest. Katey had one hand on her, yet Carolina was just happy to watch the other children play.

Bryce's brother-in-law Chris tossed horseshoes with Portia's husband Stan. Bryce had known Stan since high school but hadn't seen him in nearly two years. Since he'd married Diana. Katey's husband Drew moved close, gesturing with his beer to Ciara.

"She's great, Bryce. I'm happy for you."

Bryce felt that niggling voice in the back of his head shout off a warning.

"It's serious, isn't it?" Drew said, keeping his voice low.

Bryce tried to deny it to himself, but his heart wouldn't let him. He smiled. "Yeah, it is."

"Good, because if anything, we're all glad she dragged you back into the land of the living."

Bryce sent him an embarrassed smile, knowing it was the truth. He'd avoided people because he didn't want their sympathy for sorrow he wasn't feeling. He hadn't wanted questions about Diana, about their life that was really just existing together. Then Ciara walked in and his world tilted. Nothing was the same, not the house, not his daughter and definitely not him. He turned his gaze to her and smiled as she fussed with the table settings. She'd invited all his friends, and had prepared everything herself, made certain there were kiddie favorites like popcorn and juice boxes, and in the house, she even had goody bags for the kids for their trip home.

She made certain he, Carolina and their guests were happy.

Their guests.

These were her friends, too.

As if she knew he was watching her, she lifted her gaze. Her eyes went wide and she rushed around the table and threw open the grill.

Ciara waved at the smoke. "Oh Bryce, for pity's sake."

"Sorry." He began flipping the food before it scorched. "I was watching you."

"Oh, don't blame me for this. How hard is it to cook burgers?"

"That was a compliment," Bryce said dryly.

"Oh," she said, and reddened.

Drew chuckled and moved toward his wife as Bryce swept his arm around Ciara's waist. "Thank you, baby."

"For what?"

"For all of this. For doing it without help and well, just for wanting to."

"I couldn't let you get so involved with me that you lost your friends a second time."

"It's the woman, darlin', not the occasion that makes the difference."

Ciara's eyes teared. He was looking at her with such tenderness she thought her heart would cave in it was so full. She cupped his jaw, kissing him softly.

"Go Bryce," his sister shouted and they pulled apart.

"Go, do something," he said. "Before I make a complete fool of myself and drag you inside." He focused on the grill.

"Gee and I was going to watch you cook. That whole caveman thing is very erotic. Almost as good as the captain at the helm."

He groaned as the images of that night flooded his mind, the two of them rolling on the bedroom floor and unable to get enough of each other. Tonight would not come soon enough.

Leaving him to grill, Ciara sat on the edge of the pool, spinning Carolina in her little tube and watching the children. Mothers stopped conversation to watch the kids cannonball into the water, or stand on their hands. The men talked near the grill, passing around a bowl of chips.

Bryce said something to his sister. She laughed and

tossed him a tart smile. Ciara wasn't really listening, but watching, absorbing, the love between the brother and sister so apparent. Bryce adored his little sister. Hope was nosey because she loved him and wanted him to be happy. It made Ciara long for her own family and she wondered what they were doing right now.

How old were Mike's boys now? And had Cassie fallen in love yet? Had she had her heart broken when there was no one there who understood and could help soothe it? And Richard, she'd missed his wedding. She'd been so angry with them all for forgetting she'd existed. That she'd had plans.

Before it had been as punishment, anger, now she was the only one suffering.

"Hope, would you watch Carolina for me? I need to check on something," she said and Hope nodded, slipping into the water beside the baby.

Ciara grabbed a towel, wrapping it around her damp suit as she walked into the house. She didn't stop until she was in the bedroom she'd used when she first arrived.

Removing her computer from inside her suitcase, she didn't stop to think what she was doing, that she could be creating trouble for herself. She linked the computer across the world, through Ireland, Bangkok, Bombay and she watched the indicator take it back to Georgia, only a couple hundred miles away from where she was now.

She dialed in the number and her heart thundered as she waited for the pickup. She wanted to hear a voice from the past. Just for a moment.

"Caldwell's," a man's voice said on the other end of the line.

Ciara felt a rush of emotions.

"Hi. Ah…" She swallowed, trying to gather her composure.

"Who is this?"

"Richard?"

"Yes."

"It's me, Ciara."

There was silence and then, "Oh God. Ciara?"

"I know. It's been a while."

He scoffed and she could almost hear the bitterness in his tone.

Voices rumbled in the background and Ciara fought a flood of tears. Another voice came on. "Ciara? Oh Lord, girl. Are you near?"

Michael, she thought. Sweet dark-haired Michael. "No, I'm not. I just had to… I miss you."

"Yeah right, so much that you haven't called in what? Five years."

"Can it, Richard," Mike said. "Sugarbear, are you coming home?"

Ciara closed her eyes, realizing how much pain she'd caused her family, realizing that she'd left scars on them for the past years and they might never heal.

"I can't."

"Good grief, sugarbear, it's been years," Mike said.

"I know. I'm sorry. Is Cass there?"

"No, she's not," Richard said. "She followed your pattern and took off to parts unknown. Though she at least comes home occasionally." In the background Ciara could hear children and the voices of women.

One was reprimanding Richard and making no bones about how she felt about the way he was treating his sister. She didn't blame Richard.

"I'm causing trouble, I'm sorry. I have to go."

"No, Ciara wait," Richard said into the phone and she could tell he was holding it close to his mouth. "Just come home, baby girl, we'll fix it."

She choked and her next words came on a sob. "Bye. I love you all."

Ciara cut the line, and clutched the phone to her chest, weeping quietly and wondering if she could ever go home. Or if she'd ever have one of her own. She put away the phone and computer before she went into the bathroom to freshen up and disguise the look of a good cry.

No, it wasn't a good one, she thought. It wasn't enough. Her oldest brother's anger was justified, and she wondered about the people she'd hurt because of her career. About to leave the room, she stepped near the window, gazing down at the people enjoying the beautiful day.

Her gaze focused first on the baby, then on Bryce. He laughed with Drew, tipping his head back and she could almost feel his delight seeping under his skin. Oh, I love that man, she thought. She was happy here. She felt fulfilled and needed and wanted. She had real friends with real honest normal lives and she was liking normal so much that she considered whether or not being an agent for the CIA was worth losing this kind of happiness.

In the next breath she knew it wasn't.

Bryce tasted her, loving how she sank her fingers into his hair, how her body flexed like a silken ribbon as pleasure filled her. She moaned his name, whispering for him to come to her now. And Bryce rose from between her thighs, smiling as she beckoned him into her arms.

She climbed onto his lap, sinking down on his arousal and wrapping her arms around his neck.

For a moment he just held her tightly, feeling her fingers dig into his skin. The soft shudder that wracked her body. She tipped her head back and kissed him, slow and thick, her hips rocking against his as he filled her smoothly, pushing deep into her warmth and feeling her tender muscles grip him.

His blood pounded, his arousal throbbing and yet she moved slowly, in control, torturing him.

Ciara.

She smiled slightly, pushing his hair off his brow and watching her motion before bringing her gaze back to his. Her breath came in short quick gasps and he knew she was near. Her body was alive with sensations and he could feel each one, savored them as they matched his own.

Nothing could touch them here, he thought and swore nothing would keep them apart.

Her movements quickened, the slow seductive lovemaking turning to raw passion, primal. He loved it.

She rode him, her hips thrusting harder and harder and Bryce thought he'd come apart in pieces any second.

"Bryce," Ciara whispered. "Don't let me go."

"I won't, baby, I won't." He held her, cupping her buttocks in one broad palm and pushing her into him.

Ciara felt her heart catapult and threaten to split her chest. Heat and that delicious tension tightened her muscles, clamping him to her, gripping him with sweet friction. She cradled his face in her hands, watching her world rip apart and come together in his eyes. He rose off his haunches and jammed her down, her legs clamped around his hips and pulling him harder to her.

He chanted her name as they clung, suspended in a pool of pleasure, absorbing the tide of sensation battering them before it slid quietly away.

Bryce sank down on the bed, and Ciara looked at him, their bodies still locked.

"What is it, darlin'?" She looked scared all of a sudden.

Her gaze swept his handsome features. She licked her lips. "I love you," she said, her throat raw. "I love you. I love your baby, I love your friends."

"You do?"

Her smile was small and tight.

"It's okay if you don't love me. I know you had it rough with—"

"Hush," he said rolling her to her back. "I haven't ever said this to a woman—"

"Don't," she said, clamping two fingers over his lips. "Don't you dare say it if you don't mean it, Bryce Ashland, or I swear I'll kick your butt."

He grinned. "I just bet you will."

Shifting to his side he gazed down at her, his fingers toying with a lock of her hair. Bryce didn't feel fear or reservations, all he felt was the emotions he'd bottled up for so long.

He took a deep breath and said, "I love you, Ciara."

Tears wet her eyes and she traced her finger across his lips over his cheeks. One tear rolled down her cheek and stole his heart.

"Aw, honey."

"No one's ever loved me Bryce. No one."

"I do, darlin. I really, really do."

She kissed him and they sank into each other, and Ciara swore, at this moment, she'd never been happier.

Bryce stared lazily out the window of his office when he should be working. Yet his mind wouldn't rest. For the past week, he'd been reluctant to leave his own house and the woman within. He didn't think it was legal to be this happy, he thought. Ciara occupied his every thought and he wondered if everyone who was in love felt this way, then he didn't care. He had what he'd thought was impossible and now he had plans to make, big plans, he thought as he glanced down at the velvet box lying on his desk

He had to do this right. Because he wanted it to be memorable but he knew that Ciara had little love in her life. She seemed to absorbing all she could, storing it up and when she'd told him about walking out on her family, he'd realized she was more alone than he ever was. And he planned on correcting that soon. But for now, he had a future to start, he thought, and was about to reach for the box when someone popped into his office.

"Mr. Ashland," Bryce's secretary said in her usual low tone. "There's a call for you on line three."

"Ciara?"

Lisa smiled, amused. "No sir, someone named Steve Hartlan."

Bryce's features tightened and he nodded. As she left, he stared at the blinking light on the phone. He'd forgotten all about that. When Ciara had first started working for him, before their relationship had changed, he'd called in a few favors, asking an old friend to run a check on her. As a father, he had every right to check his new nanny's background.

His mind filled with the images of Ciara and he swore his love for her grew. He almost couldn't breathe when he thought of her, and he didn't want anything to change between them.

And he wondered if this phone call would make a difference.

He almost called Lisa back into his office to tell the caller he wasn't in, but he owed Steve the courtesy. Bryce hesitated, clamping his eyes shut and hoping to God that Ciara didn't learn about this. She'd never forgive him, but Bryce decided that for the sake of their future, he had no choice. Why was he so damned suspicious? Was it because she'd been that way from the start? Or that because she was telling him things about her past, yet still keeping the past several years in a vague scenario of traveling around the world? She'd mentioned something like eating Moroccan food in Tripoli and when he'd pursued it, she'd given him a response that was so generic, he couldn't accept it.

The thought of her lying to him twisted in his gut. He'd given her no reason to, tried to make her feel that she could trust him. He wanted to start a life with her. And if she wasn't going to help them get there, then he'd do it himself.

He reached for the phone and punched the button. "Hello, Steve."

"Hey buddy. Boy, did you ever ask for a big favor."

"Really, how so?"

"Well, there is nothing on this Ciara Stuart. I spelled it five different ways, ran her description through and nothing. At least nothing I could find."

Bryce frowned. Steve had connections to databases that included FBI and Interpol. "What do you mean?"

"I mean I hit dead end after dead end, buddy. According to records, Ciara Stuart doesn't exist."

"Did you try the first name alone?"

"Yes, and I got about fifteen million women with that name. Want to come down here and look through the files?"

"No. That *was* the favor."

"Listen, Bryce. I don't know who she is to you, but I'd be asking a lot of questions."

"Oh, I will. Believe me."

Bryce thanked Steve, said goodbye then hung up. He picked up a pen tapping it against his lips, then a moment later, he tossed it aside and left the chair.

"I'll be out for the rest of the day," he said to Lisa as he walked through the reception area.

"But sir, you have appointments."

"Cancel them," he growled as he strode out the door.

He would find Ciara, and learn all he needed. Now.

* * *

Bryce found her in Carolina's bedroom, her arms filled with his daughter. She was swaying back and forth, singing "Nothing Could Be Finer," as she lulled his baby into her nap. His heart nearly broke at the sight and he hated to be thinking what he was thinking.

She'd lied. And she'd lied from the start.

She laid the baby down in her crib, and swept a light blanket over Carolina, pausing to touch her hair.

His chest felt suddenly tight, his heart beat hard.

She turned and saw him and her smile caught him in the chest like a hammer. She came to him, kissing him. Bryce grabbed her against him devouring her mouth wanting his suspicions to leave him alone and let him have this bit of happiness. He told himself he didn't care, but he did.

He hated it, but he did.

"Whoa," she whispered when he drew back.

Then she frowned at his harsh look.

"What's wrong?"

He didn't say anything and grabbed her hand, dragging her down the hall to the master bedroom.

"Okay, now I know." She laughed softly.

"No, you don't."

"Bryce?" She pulled free and he swung around to face her. The hard look on his face sent claws of trepidation up her spine. "Why are you acting this way?"

"Ciara," he said in a low voice, grasping her by the arms and dragging her close. "I want a life with you, I want more than just this temporary feeling like I'm going to lose you any second."

"You won't."

"Then tell me what you've been hiding."

She gazed into his eyes and knew it had come, that moment.

Ciara fought the harsh reality encroaching on her heart.

The look on her face made his shoulders sag and he whispered, "Can't you trust me with whatever it is that's eating at you? I can see it, baby, you try to hide it, but I can feel it."

She pressed her head to his chest. "Oh, Bryce."

He rubbed his hands over her back, thinking she might be witness protection, and awaiting the trial. "Trust me, baby."

She tipped her head back, going up on her toes to kiss him. "Okay."

He let out a long sigh. "Tell me what's going on."

She stepped back and met his gaze. "I'm trusting you with this when it could mean my life."

Witness, he thought. He was sure of it.

"I work for the government," she said.

His features sharpened. "No, you don't."

Her brows shot up. "I thought you wanted the truth?"

"I do."

"Well this is it, I work for the government."

"How can you when there is no record of you?"

She paled, her features going slack.

"There's nothing on Ciara Stuart. No social security card, no job record, taxes, nothing on you."

"Oh God," she whispered as the realization hit her. "You had me investigated."

Bryce tensed and bit out, "Yes."

"How much investigating did you do?"

Bryce scowled at the horror in her expression, the way her voice trembled.

"How much?" she shouted when he didn't answer right away.

"When you first came here, I asked a friend to check you out. I'd forgotten about it 'til he called today. But it was a deep enough search to know that on paper, you don't exist."

She cursed and rushed from the room, her bare feet slapping the wood floors as she ran down the hall to her bedroom. Throwing open the closet she reached for her suitcase, pulling it out and tossing it on the bed.

"You're leaving? Now, without talking?"

"No, I'm not leaving. But you have no idea what you've done," she said and unzipped the case, pulling out her computer and phone, then shoving the suitcase aside to sit on the bed.

He grasped her hands, stopping her. "Why don't you just tell me?"

"You asked me to trust you, Bryce. So I am. With my life."

His features went taut. "What are you saying?"

She opened the laptop, booting it up and plugging in the phone. "That your little investigation could get me killed."

Twelve

Fear lanced through Bryce as he watched her fingers glide over the keys and was struck speechless as he recognized equipment that was not on the market, not offered to the average citizen. He watched the screen, the red line hopping over the U.S. across the sea and bouncing over three continents, then back across the ocean. *She's routing a phone line,* he thought and considered where she'd learn that. And why. The red marker stopped somewhere in Virginia.

Instantly he knew she was calling government headquarters in Langley, Virginia.

An icy foreboding crawled up his spine and it could mean only one thing. One option he'd never have suspected.

She wouldn't look at him as she spoke into the phone.

"Patterson," her boss said on the line.

"Indigo Alpha 4-0-8. Scramble the line."

Ciara was shaking, panic like she'd never experienced battering her as she waited for the appropriate clicks, counting them in her mind.

"Is he in?" she demanded when the scramble was in place.

"Where the hell have you been? I've been trying to reach you. Where are you?"

"Never mind where I am, *is he in?*" she nearly shouted into the phone, coming to her feet and pacing.

"Yes, he's locked up tight, but you have to come in, too."

Ciara shoulders sagged and she shoved the keyboard aside and rubbed her face. Thank God. "I will."

"Now. That was very clever to send the tape to the senator and the letter to me. Didn't trust me, Caldwell? That hurts."

"Too bad. My life was on the line. I had reason not to trust a single soul."

Without the willpower to stop herself, she lifted her gaze to Bryce. Her heart broke. He was glaring at her as if he wanted to grab her by the throat.

"You have to come in and be debriefed and…"

"I'm well aware of the routine, sir," she snapped. "But no, not now."

"That was an order, Caldwell."

"Then I will have to disobey it, sir."

Patterson grumbled on the other end of the line, then conceded. "All right then, when?"

"I don't know when, dammit, just give me some time." She hung up, disengaging the phone line that connected across the world. She closed the laptop and tossed the phone aside.

Silence stung the air between them and Ciara breathed deeply, trying to calm herself when her nerves were raw. She turned her gaze to Bryce. "I can't believe you had me investigated."

"Why not?" He glared. "Your entire life is nothing but damn secrets!"

"Yes, it is. It *was.*"

Ignoring her response he said, "Just what agency are you with? FBI, CIA, NIS?"

Ciara went to her suitcase, flipped it open, and pulled the bottom liner free. Then with a knife hidden there, she cut open the next layer and pulled out a black leather envelope. She opened it, handing him a familiar looking single-fold leather wallet like the one he'd carried in the Secret Service.

He flipped it open and scanned it. CIA.

He cursed.

She winced and felt the precious world she'd hidden in begin to crumble.

"Caldwell. That explains why I couldn't find anything on you." He tossed her the wallet. "You even lied to me about your name!"

"I had to. I was protecting myself as much as anyone around me."

"We were nothing but your cover," he said, appalled.

"No," she said firmly. "*No.* I didn't expect you to be here. You know that."

A spot in him agreed, but he was too furious to acknowledge it.

"You could trust me with your body, Ciara. With

your heart, but not with your life? I could have helped you.''

"No, you couldn't.'' His gaze hardened like sharp blue glass. "Bryce, listen.'' She made to touch him, but the dark look in his eyes stopped her. "My partner was working a deal with the wrong side. I saw him do it and got it on film. After covering my back, I turned it in and had to hide 'til they could catch him. Or he would have come after me.''

"Or Carolina, or me?''

"No. You weren't in danger.''

"And if this plan of yours went bad and your partner got close to you, he would have gotten close to my baby!''

"I would have died to protect her,'' she said fiercely.

"*I* can protect her, dammit, and if not for you and your lies, I wouldn't have to!''

"I was trying to stay alive. I couldn't trust anyone.''

"Not even me? Why not me, Ciara?''

There was a plea hidden beneath his anger, hurt and wounded and wanting so badly to be soothed. "Oh honey, I wanted to, but I knew you would react like this. That day at the store proved it. You asked me to trust you, and now that I am you're screaming at me, cutting me out.''

His expression turned frosty and Ciara felt the distance between them grow. "Was Katherine Davenport in on this?''

"She gave me the job. She doesn't know why I wanted it.''

"Does she know what you are?''

What you are, reverberated in her mind. Like a creature, a thing, she thought, and could see his love for her dying before her eyes.

"Yes. But not even my own family knows."

"So you left them to be a spy," he said, disgusted. "To use people, to use me."

"Yes, I did. But I wasn't using you. And you know it. It was *my* life I was trying to protect. Mark Faraday has seven years experience on me. He could have found me if he knew I'd turned him in. And if he had, he'd have killed me," she said, looking away.

"How could you be so sure?"

She brought her gaze back to his. "Because that's what I would have done."

His expression turned to granite, unfeeling, unmoving, and Ciara saw her past coming back to bite her.

"This was too serious to keep from me Ciara. I can't believe I didn't see this coming."

"You weren't supposed to."

"Yes, you're damn good, I'll give you that."

She winced. "None of us were in danger until you started snooping around in my past."

"It isn't your past, is it? You're still CIA. Do you even know who you are?"

His words cut deep, making the muscles in her chest tighten painfully and threaten her breathing. "I thought I was the woman you loved."

His features twisted with more pain.

"Apparently I'm not even that."

When he didn't say anything, Ciara knew. She knew. She'd never gain his forgiveness. So she did the only thing she could to save a little dignity. She turned around and walked out of the room.

Bryce didn't watch her leave. He didn't have to. He could feel the loss seeping through him and stealing his air.

He sank down onto the bed, cradling his head in his hands. Oh God.

Ciara walked through the stone arch of the George Bush Center for Intelligence and didn't feel what she expected. It wasn't coming home, it didn't make her feel as if she were embarking on an adventure. It simply felt foreign. Her heels clicked on the marble floor as she walked down the hall, making a series of turns, riding an elevator and stepping into the almost sterile forbidding environment.

She'd spent three days debriefing her superiors, the senator and, unfortunately, the director. She refused to tell them where she had been for the past two months until she had a promise from them not to speak with Bryce. She wouldn't involve him more than he was. She wouldn't let them destroy his life anymore than she had. She stilled, pressing her hand to the wall and catching her breath. Oh God this hurts, she thought and forced back the tears.

She continued down the hall, pushing past the double doors and into her boss's office.

He barely glanced up. "Caldwell, I'm busy," Patterson barked.

"Good. This will only take a moment."

Bryce rushed into his daughter's room and found the new nanny pacing the floor, the baby in her arms.

The young blond woman looked at him. "I'm sorry

we woke you, sir. She keeps waking and crying out
for her mama.''

''I know,'' he said, coming close and taking Carolina. ''Go back to your room. I'll take care of her.''

The nanny frowned softly, then nodded, and left
them alone.

Bryce sat in the small rocker, and cuddled his
daughter close. She settled a little, still whimpering
and clinging fiercely to him. She was too young to
understand anything beyond the fact that the woman
who'd acted like her mother was gone. It was cruel.
And Bryce blamed himself. He done what he'd sworn
he wouldn't do. Ciara had finally trusted him, and he
let her down by rejecting her. By pushing her out of
his life. She was a strong independent woman. She'd
been alone for years, taking care of herself and the
fate of the world. Of course, she would solve her
problems herself. And for the hundredth time he wondered where she was, what she was doing.

She'd left him before he'd roused himself from the
bedroom. He'd caught a glimpse of her as she'd
pulled out of the driveway. Of the tears streaming
down her face. Later he'd found her bedroom stripped
and a short note that said she'd called Wife Incorporated and they'd send someone over to help him
with the baby in the morning.

As if she could be so easily replaced.

With one look at his house and his baby, he knew
she wasn't all spying and CIA. Yet he couldn't help
the thoughts that plagued him. That he would never
be enough for her, that he and his boring life could
never replace the intrigue and danger of being an

agent. Hadn't he resented leaving his career for Diana? How could he expect that of Ciara?

He rubbed his face, his throat locking tight. Yet without her in his life, in his arms, it just hurt.

Ciara came around the side of the house and stopped, simply watching her family. She hadn't called, afraid they would shut her out. And she wanted to run, yet forced herself to take steps forward and push open the tall gate. It creaked as it swung and several faces turned toward her. She stepped out from under the shade of the wisteria bush and waited.

"Sugarbear?" Michael said, moving toward her.

She nodded.

From the far side of the yard, a young dark-haired woman shrieked and bolted toward her. Michael swept Ciara up in his arms first and hugged her. The instant he put her down, Cassie threw herself into her arms, sobbing. Ciara fought the tears and failed.

Then a deep voice said, "What do you have to say for yourself?"

Cassie let Ciara go and Michael stepped back, eyeing his older brother and not hiding his tears of joy.

Ciara looked up at Richard. "I'm sorry."

His expression faltered. They stared, then Richard walked closer and slowly closed his arms around her. "It's okay, Ciara. You're home now. All is forgiven."

"Bryce called me, looking for you," Katherine Davenport said as she handed Ciara the glass of iced tea.

The glass shook in her hand, ice cubes tinkling. "What did he want?"

Kat eyed her. "To talk to you."

She shook her head, setting the tea aside. "I can't see him, Kat. It hurts too much."

"Better safe than sorry, is that it?"

"You didn't see the look in his eyes, the disgust. Bryce hates me. And he has good reason."

"Did leaving the company mean you had to leave your backbone behind?"

Ciara scowled. "What the heck does that mean?"

"It means you went after what you wanted when you joined the CIA. Why stop there? Go for what you want now."

Ciara moved to the large window of Katherine's home that offered a spectacular view of the intercoastal waterway. "What I want isn't out there, Kat. Not for me. Not anymore."

"You sure?"

"Oh yeah. I just wanted peace and quiet and routine. Routine was so nice," she said sadly. "I want carpools and ballet lessons, and...my own babies." She choked. "I had it, Kat. I had it all, but it wasn't really mine to keep. And I'm the only one to blame for destroying it all."

"I wouldn't say that, darlin'."

She spun around, her heart slamming against the wall of her chest. *Bryce.*

"Is it true you left the agency?"

She nodded as everything about him came crashing in on her. The deep blue of his eyes, the way his dark hair fell across his forehead. The way he could look at her and make her heart stop.

"Why?"

"I couldn't do it anymore. I took one look at the gun and holster and knew that was the old Ciara. That life belonged to the woman who walked in your doors." She took a breath. "Not the woman who walked out of them."

"I see." Bryce couldn't take his eyes off her. The past week had been horrible, like he was under water, everything muffled, heavy, numbing with cold. Hurting for air. And now he felt as if he'd just shot to the surface. Looking at Ciara, it was like breathing again.

"I'm so sorry I deceived you, Bryce," she said suddenly. "But it was part of my job, I had—"

"I know. It took me a while, but I know you were protecting us." He shoved his hands deep into the pocket of his jeans. "I've made some mistakes too, Ciara. The first one was that I didn't know what I had in Hong Kong 'til it was gone."

Her lips curved with old memory.

"The second was last week when I pushed you away." He took a step closer and Ciara's breath caught. Several inches from her, he gazed into her eyes and said, "I was a fool."

"No, you were only—"

"I was," he said more firmly. "I did what you were so afraid I'd do. The instant I had your trust, I pushed you away. But finding out who you really were made me feel as if you didn't need me. That we were just a job to you."

"Oh Bryce, no."

"You're an amazing woman," he said, his gaze drifting over her face, her hair before meeting hers again. "I was afraid I wasn't enough for you. I know what that kind of life is like, how could I offer you more?''

''You already did. You offered a rope to a drowning woman, a woman so isolated she'd forgotten how to really live and love.''

''I can't give you all that intrigue.''

Hope sprang through her. ''I don't want it.''

''All I can offer is me. Painfully normal. Is it enough for you?''

She nodded, unable to speak for the thick knot crowding her throat.

He touched her face, sliding his hands into her hair and drawing her close. ''I love you, Ciara. I've missed you so much,'' he said. ''I don't care what you did before. I don't care what name you used. I only want it to end with Ashland.''

She covered his hand with her own. ''I love you,'' she whispered fiercely.

''Then come home with me, baby,'' he murmured. ''Come back to *River Bend* and marry me.''

Bryce held his breath.

''Yes,'' Ciara said on a sigh and tipped her head. ''Oh, yes.''

He kissed her, drowning in her taste, her scent, and knowing for the rest of his life he'd never get enough of her. Before she walked into his life, he'd been lost, wandering, until she stepped in and gave him a second chance to do it right.

He couldn't wait to get started.

''Hey, someone wants her share,'' Kat said.

They parted, stealing another quick kiss before Ciara looked up as Katherine strolled in, Carolina in her arms. The baby took one look at her and shrieked, reaching for Ciara.

"Mama!" she cried and Kat set her to the floor. Carolina trotted up to her and Ciara scooped her in her arms, hugging their daughter.

Normal never looked so good, Ciara thought, pulling Bryce close, breathing in his scent, stroking the baby's hair. A glorious peace settled over her and Ciara held tight, thanking God for the chance.

For a life that was so normal, it was pure heaven.

Epilogue

Five years later

"**O**h an agent would never enter a building like that," Ciara said, pointing to the TV screen and stuffing popcorn in her mouth.

"Really, mama?" Carolina said and Ciara looked down where her daughter was tucked to her side.

"Yes, honey. See," she pointed again. "He'd come in from the right side and—"

"You spoil it for us, you know."

She looked at Bryce, handing him the bowl of popcorn. "Oh, who spoiled *In the Line Of Fire* for us last week, huh?"

Smiling guiltily, he set the bowl aside and crawled into the bed, snuggling his wife into his arms, and running his hands over her rounded belly.

"That's what you get for being a secret agent," he whispered.

She tipped her head. "I'd rather be your plain old wife any day."

"Baby, there is nothing plain about you. Never will be." He kissed her tenderly, his warm hands riding over her belly. He couldn't wait to hold their baby, see Ciara in the child's features.

"I love you," she whispered.

He met her gaze. "I love you more."

She smiled and settled back against him, Carolina drifting off to sleep beside her.

Bryce sighed back into the mound of pillows and didn't think his life could get any better. He tightened his hold around his family as he thought back, to that one fanciful night ten years ago.

When destiny collided.

And that the wild explosion of it was still showering him in a blanket of the sweetest love.

* * * * *

presents

DYNASTIES: THE CONNELLYS

A brand-new miniseries about the Connellys of Chicago,
a wealthy, powerful American family tied by blood to the
royal family of the island kingdom of Altaria.
They're wealthy, powerful and rocked by
scandal, betrayal…and passion!

Look for a whole year of glamorous and
utterly romantic tales in 2002:

Where love comes alive™

Visit Silhouette at www.eHarlequin.com

SDDYN02

If you enjoyed what you just read,
then we've got an offer you can't resist!

Take 2 bestselling
love stories FREE!

Plus get a FREE surprise gift!

Clip this page and mail it to Silhouette Reader Service™

IN U.S.A.
3010 Walden Ave.
P.O. Box 1867
Buffalo, N.Y. 14240-1867

IN CANADA
P.O. Box 609
Fort Erie, Ontario
L2A 5X3

YES! Please send me 2 free Silhouette Desire® novels and my free surprise gift. After receiving them, if I don't wish to receive anymore, I can return the shipping statement marked cancel. If I don't cancel, I will receive 6 brand-new novels every month, before they're available in stores! In the U.S.A., bill me at the bargain price of $3.34 plus 25¢ shipping and handling per book and applicable sales tax, if any*. In Canada, bill me at the bargain price of $3.74 plus 25¢ shipping and handling per book and applicable taxes**. That's the complete price and a savings of at least 10% off the cover prices—what a great deal! I understand that accepting the 2 free books and gift places me under no obligation ever to buy any books. I can always return a shipment and cancel at any time. Even if I never buy another book from Silhouette, the 2 free books and gift are mine to keep forever.

225 SEN DFNS
326 SEN DFNT

Name	(PLEASE PRINT)	
Address	Apt.#	
City	State/Prov.	Zip/Postal Code

* Terms and prices subject to change without notice. Sales tax applicable in N.Y.
** Canadian residents will be charged applicable provincial taxes and GST.
  All orders subject to approval. Offer limited to one per household and not valid to
  current Silhouette Desire® subscribers.
® are registered trademarks of Harlequin Enterprises Limited.

DES01   ©1998 Harlequin Enterprises Limited

**Where royalty and romance
go hand in hand...**

The series continues in Silhouette Romance
with these unforgettable novels:

HER ROYAL HUSBAND
by Cara Colter
on sale July 2002 (SR #1600)

THE PRINCESS HAS AMNESIA!
by Patricia Thayer
on sale August 2002 (SR #1606)

SEARCHING FOR HER PRINCE
by Karen Rose Smith
on sale September 2002 (SR #1612)

And look for more Crown and Glory stories in
SILHOUETTE DESIRE starting in October 2002!

Available at your favorite retail outlet.

Where love comes alive™

COMING NEXT MONTH

#1447 IN BLACKHAWK'S BED—Barbara McCauley
Man of the Month/Secrets!
Experience had taught loner Seth Blackhawk not to believe in happily-ever-after. Then one day he saved the life of a little girl. Hannah Michaels, the child's mother, sent desire surging through him. But did he have the courage to accept the love she offered?

#1448 THE ROYAL & THE RUNAWAY BRIDE—
Kathryn Jensen
Dynasties: The Connellys
Vowing not to be used for her money again, Alexandra Connelly ran away to Altaria and posed as a horse trainer. There she met sexy Prince Phillip Kinrowan, whose intoxicating kisses made her dizzy with desire. The irresistible prince captured her heart, and she longed for the right moment to tell him the truth about herself.

#1449 COWBOY'S SPECIAL WOMAN—Sara Orwig
Nothing had prepared wanderer Jake Reiner for the sizzling attraction between him and Maggie Langford. Her beauty and warmth tempted him, and soon he yearned to claim her. Somehow he had to convince her that he wanted her—not just for today, but for eternity!

#1450 THE SECRET MILLIONAIRE—Ryanne Corey
Wealthy cop Zack Daniels couldn't believe his luck when he found himself locked in a basement with leggy blonde Anna Smith. Things only got better as she offered him an undercover assignment…as her boyfriend-of-convenience. Make-believe romance soon turned to real passion, but what would happen once his temporary assignment ended?

#1451 CINDERELLA & THE PLAYBOY—Laura Wright
Abby McGrady was stunned when millionaire CEO C. K. Tanner asked her to be his pretend wife so he could secure a business deal. But after unexpected passion exploded between them, Abby found herself falling for devastatingly handsome Tanner. She wanted to make their temporary arrangement permanent. Now she just had to convince her stubborn bachelor he wanted the same thing.

#1452 ZANE: THE WILD ONE—Bronwyn Jameson
A good man was proving hard to find for Julia Goodwin. Then former bad boy Zane Lucas came back to town. Their attraction boiled over when circumstances threw them together, and they spent one long, hot night together. But Julia wanted forever, and dangerous, sexy-as-sin Zane wasn't marriage material…or was he?

SDCNM0602